Christmas Gifts

Jan Fields

AnniesFiction.com

Books in The Inn at Magnolia Harbor series

Library of Congress-in-Publication Data
Christmas Gifts / by Jan Fields
p. cm.
I. Title
    2019953377

AnniesFiction.com
(800) 282-6643
The Inn at Magnolia Harbor™
Series Creator: Shari Lohner
Editor: Lorie Jones
Cover Illustrator: Bonnie Leick

10 11 12 13 14 | Printed in China | 9 8 7 6 5 4 3 2

1

Grace

With an ominous creak, the old wooden stepladder shifted slightly as Grace Porter climbed to the highest step she dared so she could reach the evergreen swag over the doorway to the living room.

For a moment, she wondered if she should have dragged out the taller, newer ladder they used to dust the chandelier in the foyer. Then she chided herself for being silly. She was fine. Besides, she was almost done.

Beyond where the ladder blocked the doorway, the rest of the Christmas decorations were already up in the living room, making it appear cozy and festive. Though Grace and her younger sister, Charlotte Wylde, tried to keep decorating understated so it didn't compete with the grandeur of the antebellum mansion, it took hours to bring the spirit of Christmas to the Magnolia Harbor Inn.

She'd nearly talked herself into trading ladders when she glanced down at her watch and noticed the time. It was nearly three o'clock, and their new guests were sure to come through the door at any moment. There was no time to change ladders.

From where Grace stood, she couldn't see the Christmas tree in the corner farthest from the room's fireplace. They would want a fire in there during the Christmas party, and that wouldn't mix well with a live tree.

With a resolute sigh, Grace plucked a delicate porcelain angel ornament from the box of ornaments balanced on top of the ladder. The paint on the angel had faded to pastel, and the starched lace wings scratched against the palm of her hand as she stretched to reach an open space on the greenery. Grace wondered if it would have been wiser to hang the ornaments before putting up the swag, but she'd worried about them falling off and breaking. The angel ornaments, including the tiny angel in her hand, weren't particularly valuable, but they had sentimental value, and Grace hadn't been willing to risk damaging them.

As the hook caught, Grace slowly pulled her hand away. The angel swung slightly, giving her the illusion of flight. Grace searched for any other empty spots on the swag. She hummed a Christmas carol under her breath, hoping her holiday spirit would ignite. So far, that spirit had felt far away. The inn was beautiful, but Grace had to fight the urge to sit down and have a serious pity party about how she felt this Christmas.

Spencer Lewis, her neighbor and good friend, who never let her sulk too long, was out of town and wouldn't be back before the New Year. He was spending the holidays with his daughters in Charleston. Grace was glad he had the chance to do that, but it made her all the more aware that her own son, Jake, wouldn't be able to get home for Christmas.

I can't believe I'm moping because I'm only going to be surrounded by all my other friends, family, and inn guests for Christmas. I should be ashamed of myself.

She pushed aside her gloom and focused on the task at hand. The swag was nearly full of tiny angels, but she spotted one more open spot, which was perfect as she had one last lace-winged angel.

Grace needed to scoot the ladder over a little bit to reach it more easily. She hopped down and tugged at the hem of her short-sleeved silk tee. The pink top was so pale that it was nearly off-white. Over it, she wore a warm green cardigan, knitted with cotton yarn by a friend from church. Grace thought of her outfit as Christmas colors for warm days.

She took hold of the ladder to drag it to the new position, then froze as she heard the tinkle of a bell, signaling the front door had opened. One of their guests must have arrived. Grace knew from experience that guests always paused to drink in the startling beauty of the front foyer, so she almost certainly had time to hang the last angel before she hurried to the reception desk as long as she didn't move the ladder.

"I can reach," Grace murmured as she hurriedly climbed the ladder as far as she dared with the angel ornament in her hand. She bent her knee slightly to wedge herself more securely on the ladder so she could reach out for the empty spot on the swag. "Just a little farther."

Unfortunately, the reach was about an inch too far for safety, and the ladder wobbled, threatening to raise up onto two legs. Grace squeaked in alarm.

Then she felt a strong hand on her back at the same time that someone pushed the ladder firmly back on all four legs. Shaken, Grace glanced down to thank her rescuer. She gasped.

Jake grinned up at her, his hazel eyes dancing with amusement behind his glasses. "You need to move the ladder. Physics and gravity aren't on your side."

Still clutching the little angel, Grace practically jumped off the ladder to hug her son, which actually worked well since Jake was quite a bit taller and lanky. "What are you doing here? You told me you had to stay in Raleigh for Christmas."

Jake hugged her back, his strong arms so much like his father's that it brought fresh tears to Grace's eyes. She marveled at how her little boy had grown up.

"I thought I did," he said. "But my boss rushed us all out of the office and told us not to come back until we'd made merry."

"Made merry?" Grace echoed.

"Something like that." Jake pushed a hank of thick auburn hair away from his face, then surveyed the area. "That is, assuming you have any room at the inn."

"Lucky for you, we do," Grace said. "Usually we slow down a little this time of year, but we're booked up, except for the Wisteria Loft Suite. And the only reason I have that one is because Aunt Winnie told me not to put anyone on the third floor."

Winnie Bennett was the younger sister of Hazel Wylde, Grace's late mother. She lived nearby with her husband, Gus, and she often dropped by the inn. She was always helping out her nieces, and Grace didn't know what they would do without her.

Jake raised one hand. "Scout's honor, I didn't tell her that I was coming. So why did she think you needed to keep the third floor open?"

Grace shrugged. "I don't know, but I'm glad she did. Otherwise, you'd be choosing between an air mattress or the sofa in my quarters." Then she took Jake by the shoulders. "Now let me look at you. Have you been eating?"

"Not as well as I eat here," he admitted.

Grace drank in the sight of Jake from his rumpled hair and glasses to his T-shirt that read, *Stand back—I'm going to try science!* This was the best surprise she could have imagined.

"You can study me for days," Jake said. "But I'd like to drop off this bag first." He picked up the bag at his feet and hefted it onto his shoulder.

"Oh, sorry," Grace said. "Leave it next to the reception desk, and come say hi to your aunt Charlotte."

Jake carried his luggage to the reception desk, and then Grace towed him into the kitchen.

Charlotte stood at the island nibbling on a sandwich while making one of her many lists. Not for the first time, Grace admired Charlotte's ability to keep her perfect figure when she always seemed to be sampling some new creation. The button-down shirt's tailoring showed off Charlotte's slim frame, and the rolled-up sleeves kept the cuffs from getting soaked with the many times Charlotte's hands were in water on a normal day of cooking.

Charlotte handled the bulk of the cooking at the inn, and she did an amazing job. She had been head chef at the upscale restaurant Le Crabe Fou in Charleston before she opened the Magnolia Harbor Inn with Grace. Though they offered guests only breakfast in the morning and hors d'oeuvres in the evening, Charlotte still kept her hand in the full range of creative cooking for the popular cookbooks she wrote.

The inn's resident mascot, Winston, stared at Charlotte with the focused gaze of a dog hoping it was about to rain ham.

"Merry Christmas," Jake said.

Charlotte and Winston both glanced up.

Winston barked and rushed over to greet Jake in a flurry of fluff and joyful wiggles.

Charlotte dropped her pencil and wiped her hands on her apron, then rushed to hug her nephew. "What a wonderful surprise!"

Grace smiled. "It certainly is."

"I'm glad to be here," Jake said.

"You're just in time to rescue me from overeating." Charlotte gestured to the untouched half sandwich on her plate. "Ham sandwich? The cranberry jalapeno jam on it is amazing. I bought a case of it at the farmers market last week."

"A Charlotte Wylde special sandwich?" Jake said. "You don't have to ask me twice."

"Flatterer," Charlotte scolded with a chuckle as she passed Jake her plate.

Grace opened her mouth to ask Jake how long he'd be staying, but she snapped it shut when she heard the bell over the front door chime.

"You want me to get that?" Charlotte asked.

"No, I've got it." Grace hurried out to the foyer.

A stylish young African-American woman was walking inside ahead of a tall, broad-shouldered young African-American man. He carried a duffel bag and a huge suitcase, but he showed no signs of strain from the burden.

The woman had long legs and a graceful neck that Grace often saw on models, but she wasn't as tall as the man who trailed her. She stopped near the front desk and gazed around admiringly. "This place is amazing. I think it's one of the most beautiful buildings I've ever seen. I love living in the city, but it's going to be wonderful to spend Christmas in such a quaint town."

Grace waited out the rush of words before saying, "Thank you. I hope we can make your holiday special."

The young man hiked his duffel bag farther up on his shoulder, then set the large suitcase by the woman with a noticeable thump.

The woman smiled at him. "Thank you so much."

"Happy to help," he said, though he massaged his arm, which made the woman laugh.

"Poor Isaac," she said, dropping her voice to a loud conspiratorial whisper that she directed at Grace. "I may have packed a few too many books for this trip. But I never know what I'll be in the mood to read."

"Actually, that's comforting to hear," Isaac said. "I thought she might have a person in there."

The woman laughed with an ease that suggested she laughed often.

"Welcome to the Magnolia Harbor Inn," Grace said with a smile. "I'm Grace Porter. My sister, Charlotte Wylde, and I own the inn. You must be Isaac Ryan." Since he'd booked a room for only one person, Grace wasn't sure who his companion was.

"And I'm Holly Haige," the woman said before Isaac could speak.

"I'm meeting a couple of friends here for a reunion of sorts as well as a cheering-up party for our dear Ivy. I'm sure being in such a spectacular place is going to be balm for what ails her. As I came up the front drive, I felt as if I were in a movie. It's magical. Are Ivy and Jolene here yet?"

Grace blinked as she sorted out the information she'd been offered. "No, you're the first to arrive from your group. You'll be in the Rosebud Suite. It shares a bathroom with the Bluebell Suite, but I'm certain you won't feel at all crowded. It's quite comfortable, and I trust you'll enjoy it."

"I love it already," Holly said. "I adore roses, and I saw pictures of it online. Though I have to say, the photos don't do this place justice. It has to be seen to be believed."

Grace wondered if Holly would simply keep talking until her friends arrived. She glanced discreetly at Isaac.

Already displaying a military posture, the man straightened even more when he noticed Grace's glance. "You were right, ma'am. I am Isaac Ryan. I'm here alone."

Grace couldn't help but notice that Holly's face lit up at his admission. "You'll be in the Buttercup Suite," Grace told him.

The name of the room brought a bark of laughter from Isaac that revealed strikingly white, even teeth.

"All the suites are named for flowers," Grace explained.

"That's just fine, ma'am," he said. "It'll be a nice change from a tent and a cot."

"Oh?" Holly arched her carefully styled eyebrows. "You're in the military?"

"Yes ma'am," Isaac said. "Army. Though maybe not for much longer." Then as if he regretted saying too much, he reached down and picked up Holly's suitcase. "I can carry your bag to your room."

"Thank you," Holly said.

Grace led the two of them to the stairs. "You'll find information in your rooms about local holiday events, if you're interested. We'll also be having a Christmas Eve party here for guests and family, and I hope you'll both be able to join us."

As they climbed the elegantly curving stairs, Grace went on to tell them about the complimentary wine, cheese, and hors d'oeuvres hour beginning at six. "After that, you'll be on your own for suppers and lunches. You'll find a list of excellent restaurants in your rooms. And, of course, we serve breakfast every morning."

"Sounds wonderful," Holly said enthusiastically. "But I hope the breakfast hours aren't too early. I plan to be horribly indulgent while I'm here."

Grace smiled. "I'm sure we can accommodate that."

Isaac didn't say anything as they walked, though Grace saw his expression was attentive and agreeable. He seemed perfectly content to let Holly fill in any empty space with her cheerful chatter. Grace suspected he was one of the people for whom the saying "still waters run deep" was especially apropos.

As Grace led them to the second-floor landing and gave them a moment to peer around, she glanced at Isaac. She had the feeling the young man would be challenging to coax out of his shell and made a mental note to be especially sure he had a happy Christmas.

Then Holly rested a hand on Isaac's arm and smiled at him as she remarked on the Christmas decorations, and Grace wondered if someone else could already be planning to do a little coaxing as well.

Isaac

As soon as the door closed behind Grace, Isaac dropped his duffel bag on the polished wood floor and gazed around the room. He assumed the suite's name came from the cheery yellow walls that made the space bright and sunny. The room radiated springtime in stark contrast to how close they were to Christmas, but he didn't mind at all. He had high hopes for this being a time of new beginnings, so the room seemed appropriate, if a little frilly.

Dark rose accents added to the feminine decor of the room. He regarded the pale overstuffed chair near the window and wondered if he dared sit on it.

As he ran a hand over the smooth dark wood of the king-size bed, he was suddenly struck by how much his mother would have loved this place. In his mind's eye, he saw her smiling face and the way she'd always clapped when she was delighted over something. She'd clap for the room's delicate chandelier with its lights that emulated candles. And she'd love the ruffled bed skirt and the way the room was neat as a pin. No one kept a cleaner house than his mother had.

The feeling of his mom's presence was so strong that it knocked the wind out of Isaac for a second, and he sank down onto a wooden chair.

His mother had passed away while he was overseas, and he missed her deeply. Even though he was ambushed by grief a little less often now, it still showed up, usually when he saw something beautiful. His mother would have loved to share Christmas with him at this inn. He felt sure of that. She'd have gone on and on about how proud she was. She would have wanted to take pictures of him in his uniform. And she'd have wanted to go with him when he went to the school to do his presentation.

Perhaps thinking about her smiling face would help with his already bubbling stage fright. Isaac stood and gazed in the mirror, searching for signs of his mother in his face. He knew his skin was darker. Hers had been the golden brown of sunlight shining in a forest, and his own skin was more the color of the forest shadows. His coloring was a gift from the father he didn't actually remember, a man who had died far from home when Isaac was too young to understand war and service.

"Shake it off," he told himself sternly. He took a deep breath.

He'd struggled with his feelings lately about a lot of things, including the service. He was proud to serve and follow the tradition begun by his grandfather and then his father. Being a career man had been the plan, but these last four years had been tough and made him doubt the plan. So he had important decisions to make. Maybe it was fitting that this place called up memories of his mother. She'd always helped him think through the tough decisions in his life.

"I wish you were here," he whispered.

Giving himself another mental shake, Isaac decided that action would help him focus. The service had taught him that as well. Everything felt so much harder when he had to wait, but action, even terrifying action, provided a way to push forward.

He unpacked his duffel bag. It didn't take long. Other than his dress uniform, he'd packed light. Any event that needed something other than jeans and a T-shirt was probably too fancy for him anyway.

As soon as his belongings were stowed in their proper places, Isaac went to wash his face. The bathroom was even brighter than the bedroom, with white beadboard on the walls and the same sunny yellow above the chair rail. The pedestal tub was nestled beneath a window. When he peered out the window, he saw the lake. The late afternoon sun was turning the water as golden as his bathroom, and he decided to go for a walk as soon as he could. More exercise would help him think.

The bathroom vanity appeared to be a converted dresser with a white basin sink on top. The sink reminded him of how he'd once used his helmet to hold water so he could shave when there was no sink nearby. It was amazing how many memories lay in wait everywhere he looked in this place he'd never been to before.

Isaac turned on the tap and splashed cool water on his face, then squinted up into the mirror. Water dripped off his nose as he said, "How do you do? Thank you for inviting me to speak today."

He wrinkled his nose, making more drops fall. That sounded entirely too formal. He couldn't talk that way to kids. Plus, had the kids actually done the inviting? Their teacher was probably the one who had made that decision.

Isaac groaned. Why had he agreed to talk to a class of fifth graders in the first place? He hadn't known how to deal with children even when he was one, and he doubted his skills had grown in that area over time.

Kids asked all kinds of things. They were as unpredictable as the weather.

What if they ask me if I ever saw anyone die? What if they ask me how many people have died because of me?

He shook his head, slinging off the last of the water drops before wiping his face on one of the neatly folded towels stacked nearby. Then, because neatness was as automatic to him as breathing, he folded it and hung it from the towel bar.

Isaac headed back into the larger room and began pacing beside the bed. He hadn't felt he had any choice about agreeing to come. This class of kids had saved his life. Some days, it felt as if that were literally true. Their letters full of home and hope had reminded him of why he served and had kept him grounded when it felt as if life and even sanity were crumbling under his boots.

After his mother died, Isaac had been adrift with loss, and he knew the intense grief made him dangerous to himself and the people he served with. But these children and their special teacher had helped him find his feet again.

The bed was so high off the floor that it came with a set of stairs for petite guests. Isaac didn't need any assistance as he sat heavily on the end of the bed. He reached into the pocket of his jacket and pulled out a letter. He hadn't been far from this particular letter since the day it arrived.

This was the letter that echoed in his heart and carried him through some of the hardest days of his life. And even if speaking in public made him feel sicker than facing the open countryside where any patch of scrub or dilapidated building could hide enemy combatants, the thought of the woman who wrote the words on the page was a mission he couldn't turn down.

He unfolded the paper and read the neat handwriting.

> *I've been concerned since your last letter. I know you're facing terrible things for all of us back home, and the weight of that duty cannot help but be heavy. But I believe in you. I have seen in your letters a man who is strong and brave and good.*

Isaac closed his eyes to hold back tears that suddenly threatened. Normally, he wasn't a man who cried. He fought the emotion and forced himself to keep reading.

*You've written about your hours in a church pew at your
mother's side. Do you remember the story of Moses holding
up his staff as the Israelites fought? As long as Moses held his
arms up, the battle went their way, but when he began to grow
weary and his arms sank, the battle turned. So Aaron and
Hur held up his arms to help him bear his burdens. Imagine
all of us here, holding up your arms. Everyone needs a little
support now and then. You have ours always.*

Before Isaac joined the military, he would have scoffed at the idea
of words on a page doing much to comfort him once he was the soldier
he'd determined to become.

But he knew now that those thoughts were wrong. The words of
the children's letters did make him feel better, and the wisdom and
compassion of their teacher did hold him up. Some days when he longed
to curl up into a ball and wait for the worst to happen, he pictured this
woman and the shining faces of the children as they stood next to her,
and he carried on. Their letters helped more than he could possibly
have explained to them.

"'Everyone needs a little support now and then,'" he read aloud.
"'You have ours always.'" He firmly believed that anyone who wrote
such encouraging words had to care about him.

Those words in that specific letter and the belief they stirred in
him had ignited a small flame of hope. At the other end of this journey,
Isaac hoped there would be someone who could help him decide what
his next step should be.

And maybe—just maybe—there would also be someone who
would be part of it with him.

3

Ivy

Ivy Lester motored slowly up the driveway to the Magnolia Harbor Inn, attempting to find a balance between gaping with wonder at the enormous trees that stretched toward the impossibly blue sky and carefully following the road before her. She'd been trudging to work under gray skies in Charlotte for weeks, and it didn't seem possible that anyplace could be so bright in the face of winter.

As she crept forward, she caught peeks of the inn itself, but it seemed the trees conspired against her getting a complete view until she pulled past a pair of ornamental pillars. But she found it was worth the wait when the full magnificence of the house spread before her. She pressed the brake. She simply had to stop and take in the mansion for a moment.

It was a stately building with tall white pillars drawing the eye to the verandas on the first and second floors. Ivy felt certain the verandas offered welcome shade against the South Carolina heat in the warmer seasons, allowing people to sit outside and enjoy the beauty and peace of the area. With only days until Christmas, Ivy doubted they'd need the shade much, but she welcomed the peace. Her life had been a churning emotional mess lately. She needed this. Her best friends had been right once again.

Following the curved drive, Ivy soon came to the inn's small parking area, and she slowed down, searching for a spot close to the path up to the house. She'd packed more than necessary because she was unsure of her friends' plans for her, and she needed to get her suitcase to a paved walk as soon as possible so she could roll the beast instead of trying to carry it.

Pulling into a spot, Ivy rolled down the window so she could judge whether she'd need to shrug out of her jacket. The air coming in the window was cool, probably close to sixty, but not unpleasant. Her light jacket should be fine.

She rested her hands on the steering wheel, glancing over at the house again. For an instant, she imagined Ballard Dorman in the passenger seat beside her, offering her tidbits about the architectural style of the building. *Built in 1816, the Magnolia Harbor Inn is a splendid example of antebellum mansion design.*

Ivy sighed. The information had come from the inn's website, though the voice in her head was Ballard's.

"I wish you were here," she whispered, then shook her head.

Stop wishing your life away. You can't live in the things you can't have. This time the inner voice giving her a scolding was straight from her grandmother, a woman who'd always been critical of sullen children.

A car horn jerked Ivy out of her reverie and made her jump. She twisted around, wondering if she'd parked crookedly or managed to pick a reserved space.

A sleek red sports car pulled into the spot beside Ivy.

Ivy levered out of her rather worn Mercury Milan, picked mostly because she'd loved the shade of deep blue. She squared her shoulders and prepared for whatever the driver's problem could be. Living in the city, Ivy was used to people railing at perceived driving errors.

The door flung open, almost scraping Ivy's car.

Ivy frowned, then gasped as her college friend Jolene Bettleman hopped out of the car and rushed over to engulf Ivy in a hug.

"I can't believe you're still driving this old thing," Jolene said, gesturing at Ivy's car. "Didn't you have it the last time I saw you? I've been through three cars since then."

"That's because you drive like a maniac," Ivy said. "Unless things have changed in the past few years."

"Not a bit." Jolene grinned at her, clearly not bothered in the least by Ivy's assessment of her driving. She held Ivy out at arm's length and scanned her up and down. "You're thinner, which is fine if it's the look you're going for. But it's not so good if it means you're moping instead of eating."

"You're exactly the same as I remember." Ivy knew the one way to keep Jolene from asking too many questions was to turn the conversation back to Jolene. A born storyteller, Jolene loved the spotlight. Plus, what Ivy said was true. Jolene was the same ball of fire she'd always been.

Jolene wrinkled her nose and patted her wavy red hair. "How can you say that? I'm wearing my hair different."

Ivy couldn't tell what the difference could be, but she knew better than to argue. "It's gorgeous."

Jolene smiled as she linked her arm through Ivy's. "Never fear. Holly and I will pull you out of your funk and get you back on the path to joy. This will be a Christmas to remember, and you'll return to Charlotte with your head on straight."

Jolene's unwavering surety made Ivy laugh. While the years since Ivy had last seen her friends had made her question everything, clearly the same couldn't be said about Jolene. But then again, Jolene had always been that way.

Ivy decided to keep an open mind and go along with whatever her friends suggested during their stay. Jolene could be right. This adventure could be the answer to mending her broken heart and forgetting all about Ballard Dorman.

Jolene's lively chatter kept Ivy distracted as they gathered their luggage and headed for the inn. Though the walk was short, Ivy learned about the last three guys Jolene had dated—a baseball player, a candidate for a political office in Charleston, and a guy who drove one of the carriage rides that were popular with tourists.

"I'm not limiting myself to only one guy," Jolene concluded. "That's how you avoid this kind of heartbreak. It's all about keeping things light and simple. Complexity is the thief of joy."

Ivy didn't respond to Jolene's comments, but she knew she didn't have to. Jolene would fill any pauses.

When they stepped into the antebellum mansion, they both fell silent. The foyer was dazzling from the gorgeous white marble floor to the sweeping staircase off to one side. A chandelier hung from the second floor, and the abundant sparkling prisms resembled icicles. Golden wall sconces were woven with real greenery, which gave the room a faint hint of pine scent. The entire effect was a wonderfully understated blend of holiday and elegance.

"This is perfect," Jolene said breathlessly.

Ivy had to agree with her friend.

They walked to the front desk and were met by a lovely woman whose wavy dark-brown hair hung just past her shoulders, much the same as Ivy's own. Ivy guessed the woman was in her early forties, but when they drew closer, the laugh lines at the woman's blue eyes made Ivy up her guess to the middle or late forties. The woman's figure was as trim as Ivy's, and even the cardigan she wore didn't add bulk to her figure. Ivy was in her late twenties, and she hoped she looked as good when she reached that age.

"Welcome to the Magnolia Harbor Inn," the woman said. "I'm Grace Porter, one of the owners."

Jolene dropped the handle of her suitcase and thrust out her hand. "I'm Jolene Bettleman. And this is my friend Ivy Lester. We're staying here through Christmas." She grinned. "I hope you don't mind a little ruckus."

"Don't make us sound so wild," Ivy told her friend. "You'll have us thrown out."

"Not at all. It is holiday time," Grace said easily. "I think we can manage to absorb a little ruckus."

"See? She gets me." Jolene gazed around the room and sighed. "This place is amazing. I can't lie. I envy you getting to be here all the time."

"I am definitely blessed," Grace said before deftly changing the subject. "Your friend Holly is already in her suite. Let me show you the way. I do hope you'll both join us on Christmas Eve. We're having a party for our family and guests of the inn. You'll find we all enjoy a little ruckus then. I've also left a list of local holiday events in each of your rooms."

"Holiday events?" Jolene's face lit up. "Parties?"

"There are a number of events," Grace said, a faint expression of concern touching her face. "But I'm afraid the only party is the one we're having."

Jolene's smile never dimmed. "Not a problem. Anywhere we go, it'll be a party. And there's always shopping."

"You'll find Magnolia Harbor has a number of charming shops in the historical downtown," Grace said. "One of my favorites is Miss Millie's dress shop, not far from The Book Cottage. If you're shopping for holiday party clothes, Miss Millie's is certain to have what you need."

"Wonderful," Jolene said, nearly hopping up and down. "And Holly will be glad to hear about a bookstore. For a fun girl, she really loves her books."

Grace's eyes twinkled as she said, "I understand she packed quite a few."

"It won't be enough," Jolene said. "When it comes to Holly and books, there's never enough."

"I'm sure we'll all have a great time here," Ivy offered. "I've never stayed in such a beautiful inn."

"Thank you," Grace said. "We love it."

As Grace led them upstairs, she explained that the complimentary wine, cheese, and hors d'oeuvres hour would be held in the dining room at six. "When it's warm enough, we try to have it out on the back veranda, but it's cooler today and will probably become a bit chilly as the sun sets. We're holding off making a final decision, but when you come downstairs, you should swing through the dining room. When the weather is too cold, we serve in there."

Jolene chuckled as they reached the second-floor landing. "I'd just as soon eat indoors anyway. I've never been fond of mixing food and the outdoors." She wrinkled her nose. "I can't imagine how you keep the bugs off the food."

Ivy winced at her friend's bluntness. She couldn't believe Jolene had suggested the food would be unhygienic, and she had no idea what to say to soften the remark.

"We're very careful," Grace said cheerfully. "You may find that the view of the lake from the back veranda is well worth the venture into the wilds."

Ivy nearly laughed. *Good for you.* She was glad to see the innkeeper wasn't going to let Jolene run all over her. Ivy knew Jolene meant well as always, but she could be an acquired taste sometimes.

A door flew open, and Holly ran out. "I knew I heard Jolene!"

For a long moment, Ivy and her friends did a lot of hugging and squealing.

As Jolene and Holly gushed over each other's outfits, Ivy simply basked in the presence of the two people she had always been completely comfortable with. At one time, they'd been as close as sisters, and Ivy was glad to slip into the warmth of their relationship again. Jolene could be too blunt sometimes, and Holly could talk the ears off an elephant, but they were the two people Ivy knew better than anyone else. They understood her secrets and her heart, and they'd always offered a safe place for both.

Finally, the three quieted, and Ivy apologized to Grace, who had waited silently through the reunion. "We shouldn't hold you up. We have days ahead for catching up."

"I don't mind," Grace said, her smile kind. "It's always a delight to fill the inn with that kind of friendship and joy. But if you're ready, I'll be happy to show you to your rooms."

"Can you show me mine first so I can dump these bags?" Jolene asked. "I want to see this fabled Dogwood Suite. I will honestly admit to drooling a little at the photos you have online."

Ivy felt her face warm. "You guys know I feel bad about taking the biggest suite."

Holly waved off the remark. "You're the one here to heal. That takes space. And I can tell you right now that I love my room."

"You deserve some luxury," Jolene added, patting Ivy's shoulder. "And I understand the Dogwood Suite has that in spades."

"We think so," Grace said. She opened the door next to Holly's room. "This is the Bluebell Suite."

Ivy peeked through the door as Jolene followed Grace inside. The room was large with walls painted the cheerful blue of its floral namesake. It featured a king-size bed with a tufted headboard. A cozy love seat faced a small fireplace. The rug under the love seat and the fireplace's tile trim echoed the blue of the walls. But the homey atmosphere wasn't without elegance, especially with the delicate crystal chandelier and polished hardwood floor. Ivy thought the biggest surprise of the room was a soaking tub on one wall.

"Oh, you know I'm going to make use of that bathtub," Jolene announced.

"There's another one in the bathroom too," Holly told her. "So I'll claim that one. And you should see the adorable rose-sprigged wallpaper in my room. I love it."

"If we leave the bathroom doors open, we can talk while soaking," Jolene said. "How fun would that be?"

Ivy was impressed that Holly seemed accepting of that idea, but then Holly and Jolene had always been the more outgoing ones of the trio. Ivy often felt as if she were bobbing along on the currents of their energy.

Jolene directed her next burst of conversation to Grace. "These rooms are better than I expected. Now let's see the Dogwood Suite."

Grace's expression had turned fondly amused, and Ivy realized that it probably mirrored her own. Though Jolene could be rather boisterous, there wasn't a malicious bone in her body, which made her easy to like in spite of her raucousness.

When Grace led the three friends to the Dogwood Suite, they met the sight with matching gasps. Ivy had also seen the photos of the room on the website. They all had. But studying a photo was never the same as being in a place. Often photos overplayed the subject, but in this case, they had done the opposite. The reality of the opulent suite was simply impossible to capture in pictures.

The Dogwood Suite's tall windows offered a full lake view that nearly took Ivy's breath away. The suite was more formal than Jolene's room and so large that it made the king-size four-poster bed seem almost small. Two overstuffed chairs clad in striped upholstery faced a fireplace with clean lines, giving the room a nice balance of timeless and modern as did the gold-and-white color scheme.

Ivy especially admired the little desk in the corner that offered a place to sit and write. Though she knew it was unusual and possibly even a bit eccentric, Ivy loved writing letters, not with a computer but with a pen and paper. She believed it conveyed more warmth, and she rather enjoyed showing off her handwriting.

"If there's nothing else you need, I'll leave you ladies to settle in," Grace said. "I hope to see you all for hors d'oeuvres this evening at six."

"We'll be there," Jolene assured her.

Once Grace was gone, Jolene walked over and hopped up on the bed. "If you get tired of this room, let me know."

A pang of guilt blossomed in Ivy's chest. "If you'd prefer this room—"

"She wouldn't," Holly said firmly, then slung an arm around Ivy. "This is for you. And anything else you need to get you through this. We're going to do whatever we can to patch up your broken heart."

Jolene snorted. "I wouldn't know about broken hearts." She pointed at Ivy. "But don't worry. We're here to help you find your way back to the joyous single life we planned for ourselves back in college. It's the only way to go." She spread her arms wide. "I've never deviated from the plan, and my life is fantastic."

Holly rolled her eyes. "We know it is. But now is not the time to hear all about it. Now is the time to help Ivy have a good Christmas."

"By embracing the plan," Jolene insisted.

Ivy didn't speak up, but she had never been truly in love with the idea of making her whole life about herself and her career. When she'd been in college, the plan had sounded empowered and bold—two things she longed to be—but somehow it had never fit her as it had Jolene. Ivy always felt as if she were trying to fill someone else's shoes.

Though she had to admit, her love life hadn't exactly been kind to her recently. So maybe Jolene was right. After all, both she and Holly were obviously doing great. Neither of them wore a strained smile, the kind that was a flimsy dam trying to hold back the sea.

"Penny for your thoughts?" Holly asked, giving Ivy's shoulders a light squeeze.

"I was thinking how wonderful you both are," Ivy said. "And how right you are. The plan clearly works, and I'm all in."

"That's my girl," Jolene said, jumping off the bed and rushing over to Ivy and Holly. She threw her arms around them, yelling, "Group hug!"

Engulfed in her friends' warmth, Ivy wished it stood a chance of warming the cold stone inside her chest.

4

Grace

Still smiling over her new guests' reunion, Grace walked down the back stairs to the kitchen. She found her sister at the center island, leaning on one elbow while she flipped through cooking magazines. Grace glanced around the room and saw Winston napping in a pool of sunlight near a window. "Where's Jake?"

"He headed up to his room." Charlotte closed the magazine and pushed it away from her. "He said there was no reason for anyone to walk him up since he knew the way."

"That's true enough, but I need to give him the list of community Christmas events. Since I didn't know he was coming, I didn't put one in his room."

"Speaking of events, I need inspiration for the Christmas party." Charlotte picked up a notepad and a pen. "I'm stuck."

"I thought we were going traditional," Grace said. "Turkey and the works."

Charlotte huffed, turning the notepad around to show her a list. "Yes, and I wrote down all the traditional elements, but there's an endless variation within that. I plan to use mostly family recipes, but I want to bring in something new as well."

"What do you have in mind?" Grace asked.

"Sort of my personal take on a classic. But I'm not sure where to inject it." Charlotte tapped the paper with her pen. "Maybe a new take on sweet potatoes. Or some unexpected vegetables."

"Well, don't tamper with the family stuffing recipe," Grace said.

"There will be an uprising if you do."

"No worries." With a sigh, Charlotte tossed the notepad and pen back on the counter. "So, you've met all our guests now. How are they?"

"Interesting," Grace replied. "I think you'll appreciate Jolene and Holly. They're both lively. Isaac and Ivy are quieter, and it's obvious that they're both carrying some heavy burdens."

"I'm sure you'll figure out how to help them," Charlotte said. "You always do."

"I believe Ivy is nursing a broken heart," Grace continued. "We'll have to make especially sure she has a wonderful Christmas while she's here."

"I appreciate the little extra pressure," Charlotte said with a smile. "But seriously, I feel terrible for her."

Grace nodded.

Charlotte checked the clock on the wall. "I need to get going on the hors d'oeuvres."

"What are you making?"

"I'm staying fairly simple tonight, but I want to hint at the festivities to come. We'll have fresh fruit and artisan cheese with crackers, and I plan to use brie in two ways. I'm going to put together cranberry brie puff pastry swirls with cinnamon sugar."

"Nice," Grace remarked. "The smell of cinnamon always evokes the holidays."

"Exactly. Then I'll use the rest of the brie to stuff some crispy baby potatoes. And I'm making some crab puffs. Do you want to help?"

"Always," Grace agreed and set to work scrubbing the small potatoes.

Charlotte took butter and brie out of the fridge to soften at room temperature. As she continued gathering ingredients for the hors d'oeuvres, she asked, "Do you think it's warm enough for the food to be served on the back veranda? I felt a distinct nip in the air when I walked over, and it's probably gotten cooler since then." Charlotte lived in a small renovated cottage located on the inn's property.

"I suspect Holly and Jolene probably won't notice the chill," Grace replied. "They seem like they're a force of nature all by themselves. But Jolene did mention that she doesn't care for eating outdoors."

"If it's warm enough, she may have to adjust," Charlotte said as she poured dried cranberries into a bowl. "The view from the back veranda is too good to waste."

"It certainly is."

"So, getting back to the menu for the party," Charlotte said. "Perhaps I could do something unique with the desserts. What do you think? Should we have a fresh take on pumpkin pie or maybe a cake?"

Finishing the last little potato, Grace set it in the bowl and pushed it toward Charlotte. "I'm sure either one would be amazing. Of course, you shouldn't forget that Winnie is planning to bring her delicious chocolate torte."

Charlotte frowned. "I suppose that will be fine. Her torte is always magnificent, but I don't want anyone else treating the party like a potluck dinner."

With a chuckle, Grace poked her sister gently. "Don't be a snob. Holiday time means we make concessions for family."

Charlotte made a face at her, but Grace knew her sister wasn't offended. Charlotte just wanted anything dealing with food to be perfect and unique.

Charlotte turned so she was leaning her back against the counter and folded her arms over her chest. "It's going to be great having Jake around for Christmas. I know you're thrilled."

"I am." Grace couldn't help but smile. "But I wish he would have told me. He gave me quite a jolt, sneaking up on me while I was on the ladder hanging ornaments."

"Speaking of which . . ." Charlotte gestured toward the stepladder leaning against the wall in the corner of the kitchen. "Is that new kitchen decor?"

Grace laughed. "I barely managed to get it this far with all our guests arriving. Plus, I still have a few Christmas decorations to hang tonight after the guests have gone out for dinner. After I finish up, I'll see if Jake will carry it upstairs for me."

"Putting him to work right away then?" Charlotte teased.

"He doesn't have to help if he doesn't want to." Grace wiped her hands on a kitchen towel. "But Jake has always enjoyed pitching in. I doubt he's changed in the time he's been away."

Charlotte didn't reply for a moment, clearly mulling something over. Finally, she said, "Did you notice anything odd about Jake?"

The question immediately sharpened Grace's mothering sensors. Had she missed something already? "No, he seemed the same as always. Did he say something to you?"

Charlotte fiddled with the bowl of cranberries, spinning it slowly. "I asked him how he was doing. He said he was a little tired because he's been working some late nights on a new project at the office."

"That seems reasonable."

Charlotte nodded, then smiled. "You're probably right." She opened a cupboard and began to dig through the spices.

Grace could tell that Charlotte hadn't believed Jake. Grace trusted her sister's instincts, but she couldn't imagine she'd missed something. She wondered what could possibly be bothering Jake. "Maybe he has a serious girlfriend and isn't sure about telling us," she mused. "He might figure we'd make a fuss."

"I don't think that's it." From the cupboard, Charlotte pulled out a tin box that held a bag of cinnamon sticks. She carried a stick over and began running it over a grater, filling the kitchen with the spicy scent as the cinnamon rained down on the dried cranberries in the bowl. "Jake would bring her home. He'd know we wouldn't mob the poor girl. He was always pretty open with his girlfriends in high school and college."

"Then what do you think it could be?" Grace asked. "Something related to his job?"

Charlotte tapped the grater against the bowl. "Well, it's possible he's been fired. He wouldn't want to tell you, especially during the holidays, because you'd worry. And it would explain his suddenly being free to come home for Christmas when he had previously thought he couldn't."

"No, he couldn't have been fired." Grace was horrified at the very thought that Jake would be afraid to tell her anything. She believed their relationship was stronger than that. "If Jake did leave that job, he'd get another one right away. He's a talented software programmer. And I happen to know the last app he helped create made the company a lot of money. It's most likely a simple explanation. He probably just wants to spend Christmas with us."

"That's surely it." Charlotte spun around and grabbed a large serving board for the fruit and cheese. "I think some sliced apples dipped in lemon and dusted with cinnamon sugar should be enough fruit along with the grapes, don't you?"

Grace studied her sister, wondering if Charlotte was placating her.

Before she could ask, the kitchen door swung open and Dean Bradley walked in. He wore a perfectly tailored black shirt, black pants, and a charcoal tie. Dean owned The Tidewater, the contemporary inn and restaurant on the other side of the lake. Many of the Magnolia Harbor guests dined at the trendy restaurant at least once during their visit.

Though just under six feet tall, Dean appeared taller because of his trim build. His good looks and infectious smile made him popular around town, but he hadn't always been popular in Charlotte's kitchen. The two chefs had matching competitive natures, and that had led to them butting heads more than once, a scenario stretching all the way back to their days of working together at Le Crabe Fou in Charleston.

Grace was glad that Charlotte and Dean were friendly now, though she suspected Dean's feelings for Charlotte might be deeper than simple friendship. Not that he had done much to give that impression, but it was something Grace felt just the same.

Regardless of any undercurrents and despite their competitive natures, Grace knew Charlotte appreciated Dean's tendency to bring a fresh perspective, which helped calm Charlotte's urge to second-guess herself. If anything, competition seemed to make her sister happier and more confident.

"I didn't see anyone at the reception desk, so I came through," Dean said.

At the sound of his voice, Winston's head shot up, and he scurried over to greet Dean.

As Dean bent down to pat the little dog, he said, "What has two of my favorite ladies all abuzz?"

"My nephew is home for Christmas," Charlotte said before Grace could answer. "His arrival was a surprise and a little mysterious, so we're trying to figure it out."

Straightening, Dean grinned at her and reached toward the bowl for a dried cranberry, which earned him a light rap on the knuckles from Charlotte. "Maybe he simply wants to spend the holidays with his mom and aunt. Or maybe he's desperate for good food."

"Which is what I said," Grace pointed out. "Well, except for the part about food, though that's a good point too. Jake can cook, but he can't make anything to compare with Charlotte's food."

"You're being dull." Charlotte plucked a grape from the bunch in the fruit bowl and threw it at Dean. "I thought you'd come up with a more interesting theory."

He caught the grape and popped it into his mouth. After chewing for a moment, he raised a finger. "Okay, I have an idea. Maybe Jake is here because he's being chased by international spies. Or maybe he's been recruited by international spies. Or maybe the guy isn't Jake at all but an international spy replacement who had plastic surgery so we won't realize he's an impostor."

As he finished his list of increasingly ridiculous ideas, Grace and Charlotte each grabbed a grape from the fruit bowl and tossed them at him.

Impressively, Dean snatched them both out of the air. "Fine. See if I help you with any future conundrum."

"I can probably live with that," Charlotte teased. She turned pointedly back to the counter and pulled the bowl of washed potatoes toward her. "Did you need something, Dean?"

He put a hand to his chest. "You wound me, Charlotte. You truly do. I came to see if I can contribute to the Christmas party. I thought maybe I could whip up a batch of your famous family stuffing to take the pressure off you. All you need to do is give me the recipe."

"You will never get that recipe." Charlotte poked him playfully before picking up a potato and a fork. "Never."

Dean laughed. "Somehow I thought you'd say that. But you can't blame a chef for trying."

Charlotte gave him a look that suggested she could definitely blame him for trying. She started jabbing the potato with the fork. "If you want to bring something, that would be all right. You could surprise us with one of your own recipes."

"I may do that," he said. "What I really came by to ask was if you're still planning to come to the charity comedy event tonight. I need to know so I can leave your name at the greeter's podium. I hope you don't mind sitting with me."

Charlotte's busy hands stilled, and she gave him a long measuring stare, which Grace knew was mostly feigned. "I suppose I could sit with you."

"You may have to," Dean said. "It's going to be packed, especially since we've had to close our normal patio dining for the show so we don't freeze our patrons. So tell your guests to call for reservations if they want to come. I can't guarantee they'll get seats otherwise."

Charlotte set the punctured potato back in the bowl before turning to Grace. "Do you mind if I go to the show? I'll probably need to leave you with the cleanup after the social hour."

"That would be fine," Grace said. "If you can spare me for a few minutes, I should run up and speak to Jake and the guests. I want to let them know about the need to call for reservations right away if they want to attend the show."

Charlotte's eyes twinkled as she ducked her head. "And I'm sure it's not an excuse so you can quiz Jake and find out more about his mysterious visit."

"There's nothing mysterious about this visit," Grace said. "And if Jake is holding back on telling me something, I'm sure he'll reveal it in his own time." She wished she felt as confident as her words sounded.

"You should make sure he's not a spy," Dean joked. "Ask him who won the World Series."

Grace put a hand on her hip. "And who did win?"

Dean shrugged. "How would I know? I'm a chef, not an athlete."

"Or maybe you're the spy," Charlotte said, grinning impishly.

"You'll never know," Dean teased.

Grace tapped her chin. "I think I'll bring him a nice hot chocolate. Nothing soothes the soul like a warm beverage."

"That's a sentiment I can get behind," Dean agreed as he reached for a grape and got another smack from Charlotte. "Hey, when are you going to fix me a warm beverage?"

"Right after I give you the stuffing recipe," Charlotte said sweetly.

5

Jake

In the Wisteria Loft Suite, Jake had changed into a well-worn sweatshirt and jersey pants, his favorite thinking clothes. He would change back in time for the social hour, but he wanted to get a little work done before then.

He pulled one of the leather chairs closer to the bed, where his laptop sat open. His sandwich plate rested on the trunk at the foot of the bed, forgotten now as he stared at the lit screen in front of him. He was at the troubleshooting stage in his coding for the new app, and it required all his attention as he pored over the information on the screen.

Some of the other programmers hated this step, feeling the degree of concentration required was tedious and boring, but Jake found it almost restful. Software coding was challenging sometimes, but ultimately it was based on logic, something life often wasn't. If he wrote the code correctly, the end result was useful and predictable. Life and people never offered those kinds of guarantees.

A notification appeared at the bottom of his screen, and Jake groaned. He was fairly sure he knew the source and content of the e-mail.

Sure enough, it was another message pressing him for an answer. He closed the e-mail without answering. "I don't have an answer," he said, then winced as his voice disturbed the quiet of the room.

A tap on the door came so soon after Jake spoke that it made him jump. He hoped no one had heard him talking to himself like a crazed relative hidden away in the attic.

When he opened the door, he found his mother standing there.

She held up two mugs of hot chocolate. "Want to share cocoa with your mom?"

"I don't know," Jake said with a grin. "Are they made from scratch or a packet?"

His mom rolled her eyes. "With your aunt in the kitchen, would I even consider making hot chocolate from a packet?"

"Good point." He motioned to the mugs. "Do they have cinnamon?"

"Fresh cinnamon. Charlotte shaved some in right on top of the whipped cream." Mom raised the mugs again. "Do they pass muster?"

"Definitely." He held the door open and stepped back so she could enter. "I miss your hot chocolate. I resort to the packaged kind at home."

"I won't tell your aunt," she said.

"That's probably for the best." Jake carefully took one of the mugs. He swung the chair back around to face the matching seat near the fireplace. "If I'd known you were coming, I'd have gotten the fire going for the ambience."

"Having you here is ambience enough, but you may need a fire for the warmth," his mother said as she pulled her cardigan closer around her. "You should have raised the thermostat when you arrived. I had it turned down since no one was booked for the room."

"I enjoy the cool air," Jake said as he settled into the chair he'd moved. "It gives me an excuse to wear a sweatshirt." Then he raised a hand. "Though I promise to change for social hour."

"You wear whatever makes you happy." Mom took a sip of the cocoa before pointing at the laptop. "Are you making this a working holiday?"

"Only a little," Jake promised. He reached over to close the laptop, not wanting his mom to see the e-mails popping up. "I promise to be completely present for all family time, but computers are my career. You can't expect me to go cold turkey."

"You work as much as you want. I can share," she said agreeably. "So how is your job going? You told me good things about your company's thingy, Gift Assistant."

"It's an app, not a *thingy*." Jake took a sip of the hot chocolate and let the rich, complex flavor overwhelm his senses for a moment. When he opened his eyes, he saw his mom smiling at him. "It's good hot chocolate. Hey, you didn't say. Did you try the app? I sent you a code for a free download."

Mom flushed. "I'm sorry, but I never used it. I never even downloaded it. I still can't be comfortable involving a computer in my gift giving."

Jake laughed. "That's why I sent you the code. I knew it wasn't anything you'd actually buy for yourself. But I promise it's a useful app. It tracks upcoming birthdays of everyone the user loads in and offers links to gifts the person will enjoy. It's been huge. The biggest seller our company has had to date."

"I'm sure it's wonderful," she said, though Jake doubted her sincerity a little. "And I hope the company appreciates you for coming up with it."

"The apps are team projects," Jake injected. "I'm only part of it, but the idea for that one did come from me." He couldn't help tooting his own horn a tiny bit. He knew his mom wouldn't think him a braggart for it.

"And you were the lead programmer," she added. "I pay attention to your e-mails."

Jake gave in. He knew she would always see him as some kind of wonder. It was a mom thing. "The company appreciates me plenty. I'm really happy there."

"I'm glad." His mother leaned back in the chair and crossed her legs neatly at the ankle while she took another sip of the hot chocolate. Though the sip was small, it left a tiny chocolate mustache that made

Jake smile. "So are you enjoying Raleigh? Do you get out much, or do you work all the time?"

"I run in the mornings," Jake said, though he winced when he said it. It had been a while, but he made a silent promise to himself that he'd return to it. "Even in the rain. Running gets me outside in the fresh air every day."

"But that's not a social activity," she argued. "Unless you run with someone. Do you have an exercise buddy?"

Jake frowned. He was far too old for his mother to worry about whether he'd had any playdates lately. "I actually prefer running alone. It's good thinking time."

Again she took a sip of the hot chocolate, and he wondered if she had something on her mind.

"Seeing anyone?" she asked.

Aha, Jake thought. *Now we get to the point.* "I date a little, but there's no one special right now. Don't worry. I'm not turning into a hermit. I do get out sometimes. In fact, a bunch of us from the apartment building had a Christmas party of our own before I left town."

"So you're happy," his mom said. "Is there anything bothering you?"

Jake wondered why his mother was asking all these questions. Had she sensed the turmoil he was feeling about the pending decision? Surely he was better at covering his emotions than that. For a moment, he wondered if he should fess up. But then he rejected the idea. He wasn't going to let his problems ruin his mother's Christmas. "Nothing's bothering me."

"I don't suppose you know any spies."

Jake sat forward, suddenly concerned. "Spies? What are you talking about? Have you been working too hard?"

She waved off his questions. "Forget it. It's just something silly that Dean said."

Jake perked up at the name. "Dean Bradley? Aunt Charlotte's archnemesis? I remember him."

"They've moved on to friends," his mom said. "Charlotte invited Dean to the Christmas party, so don't mention the archnemesis thing."

"I won't say a word," he promised. "But you can relax. I'm fine and completely free of spies these days, if you don't count the occasional James Bond marathon on TV."

They sat in companionable silence, sipping their hot chocolate and enjoying the peace and quiet of the third floor.

He wondered again if his mom's questions had come from her sensing the decision he was wrestling with. She could be positively spooky when it came to telling when someone was struggling. Once again he reminded himself that he wasn't keeping quiet because he didn't value his mom's judgment. In fact, he thought she was amazing, but he wasn't quite ready to jump into a discussion of his problems. After all, Christmas should be about Christmas.

As Jake considered the situation, he noticed his mom's gaze sharpen and knew he must be giving off worried signals. To head off any other questions, he grinned at her and said, "Please tell me we'll be having Christmas dinner with all the trimmings. I know you normally serve hors d'oeuvres in the evenings, but I've been looking forward to stuffing myself with Aunt Charlotte's roast turkey."

"We're definitely having Christmas dinner, though it's probably going to be at the Christmas Eve party," Mom said. "But Christmas Day will involve delicious leftovers."

"I can live with that."

"You should have told me you were coming. I already mailed your present to Raleigh. I hate that you'll have nothing to open at the party."

"Being with family will be present enough," Jake said. "Hey, I noticed how nice everything was decorated downstairs, but I haven't checked out the tree yet. I assume it's in the living room since you were hanging ornaments in the doorway."

"It is," she answered. "You should go see it after the social hour. Also, I could use your help getting the stepladder into the attic."

"Sure thing. Oh, did you put RoboGuy on the tree?"

When Jake was about six, he'd taken apart an old clock he found in the attic because he wanted to figure out how it worked. No one had been able to put it back together, and his mother had let him build something with the clock parts. He'd made a tiny robot, only about four inches tall. It didn't work or anything, but it looked cool with lots of cogs and wires. He knew it wasn't exactly his mom's style, but she'd let him hang it on the Christmas tree, front and center, every year.

His mom's face darkened, clearly upset. "I don't remember seeing RoboGuy when I was going through the ornaments. He must be up here somewhere in one of the storage boxes. I'll search for him."

"You don't need to go to that kind of trouble," he said. "I'm sure RoboGuy is fine wherever he is. I just happened to think of him."

"No, I can find him," she insisted. "I wouldn't have thrown him out. RoboGuy is family."

Jake laughed, but he had to admit that he was glad his mom took his rather strange creation so seriously. Plus, searching for the ornament would give her something to do other than poking around in his secret. He'd tell her when he was ready. When he knew what he intended to do.

All he had to do was figure that out.

Ivy

"I'll see you downstairs," Ivy called as she waved at her friends.

Jolene blew her a kiss while Holly smiled. They both stepped into their own rooms, leaving Ivy free to retreat to her own.

Ivy closed her door and leaned against it, sighing with relief. She'd forgotten how much being with Holly and Jolene was like standing in the middle of a storm, exhilarating and exhausting in equal measure. They never seemed to run out of energy, which was not at all like Ivy, who required time to herself to recharge.

She was glad they were so excited about catching up, but Ivy worried that their plans didn't include any of the quiet time she longed for. Even now, she would have loved nothing more than to flop into one of the comfy chairs and stare out at the lake for an hour or two, but she barely had time to freshen up before the social hour.

And she knew better than to think she could hole up in her room and sit the social part out. Jolene and Holly would come searching for her. Thankfully, her friends weren't known for their punctuality, which gave Ivy a short respite.

In the bathroom, she gazed longingly at the tub but opted for a shower instead. She was glad to find it made her feel considerably less road worn.

She wrapped a huge, fluffy towel around herself and walked to one of the two vanities, pulling off the shower cap as she went. She stared into the mirror. Without makeup, she appeared tired and sad.

Ivy darted back into her room and opened the suitcase to retrieve her hefty cosmetic bag before facing the mirror again. Though time was tight, she carefully covered up the signs of how much she was mourning the end of her relationship with Ballard. When she was done, she felt mostly successful. At least she no longer looked as if she might burst into tears at any moment.

Though she still felt like it.

As she ran a brush through her hair, she wished she had either Jolene's gorgeous red hair or Holly's amazing curls. Instead, her hair was thinner and limper than she'd prefer.

"Though the color is probably appropriate," she muttered. "Mousy brown for a quivering mess of a woman." She wondered if she should give up and go with a ponytail. At least it would pull the mess out of her face.

While rummaging around in her cosmetic bag for a hair elastic, she suddenly remembered one of the many times that Ballard had gently scolded her for being too hard on herself. "I wish you could see yourself the way I see you," he'd said time and again.

Ivy blinked back tears. "If you thought I was special, why were you out with someone else? Why aren't you here with me?"

The memory of spotting Ballard with that other woman was as sharp as broken glass in Ivy's head and heart. The woman had been perfect—stylish and elegant with a cool, effortless grace. All the things Ivy wasn't. "Are you saying those wonderful things to her now, Ballard?"

Suddenly furious with herself, Ivy scrubbed at the tears in her eyes with the heels of her hands, ruining her makeup and requiring that she start over. She was not going to keep doing this. It was Christmas, and she was spending it with two of her oldest and dearest friends. And she was going to get over Ballard and his wandering eye.

Ivy marched back into the bedroom and retrieved her phone. It was time for a fresh start. She went through her phone, deleting

Ballard's contact information, e-mails, texts, and photos. It felt good to eliminate him from her life once and for all.

Then she opened her suitcase again, promising herself she'd unpack as soon as the social hour was over. Only a few things needed immediate hanging, and she took care of that before choosing something for the evening.

Ivy slipped into a lightweight sweater in a bold shade of red that reminded her of the roses Ballard had bought her for her birthday. At the thought, she almost changed the sweater, but she knew that every item in her suitcase held some memory or other and she had to wear something. She matched the sweater with black pants and flats.

As Ivy regarded the outfit in the long antique mirror in one corner of the room, she realized Jolene was right. She had lost a little weight, but the sweater and pants combination still fit. Then she had a wry thought about the combination of red and black. "It's a little like this trip," she said to her mirror self. "Half celebration, half wake."

She spun on her heel and strode out of the room. She was going to meet this holiday head-on. And if there were any two people who could help her learn to take the world by storm, it was Holly and Jolene. "Bring it on," Ivy whispered as she trotted down the stairs.

Once downstairs, Ivy learned the social hour had moved outside after all. She was glad of her choice of a sweater, though when she stepped onto the veranda, she realized the cool air wasn't chilling. It was refreshing.

It didn't take long to spot Holly and Jolene. They stood as far from the door as possible while still being on the veranda. Jolene was giving the stink eye to an adorable little dog who was dancing around the feet of a tall African-American man. The man knelt to reach the fluffy dog.

"That dog is darling," Ivy said when she reached Holly and Jolene.

"His new friend isn't bad either," Holly said with a twinkle in her eyes. "His name is Isaac, and he's a soldier. I do admire soldiers."

Ivy expected Jolene to say something equally sassy, but instead her friend muttered, "I cannot believe they're letting a dog wander around the veranda where they expect us to eat. Isn't it enough to compete with bugs for our food?"

"Don't be such a killjoy," Holly said. "The dog is cute, and he's not begging or anything. Besides, he's not anywhere near you."

"And he'd better stay away," Jolene said. "I can't imagine getting dog hair all over my clothes. I never understood why anyone would want a big, lumbering beast in their home."

Holly laughed. "I believe you said nearly the same thing when I was dating a football player."

Ivy remembered that, and she laughed along with Holly. Jolene certainly had never minded sharing her opinion.

For a moment, Jolene glared at both of them. Then her face seemed to crack, and she dissolved into giggles. "Fine, but don't try throwing a stick and expecting him to fetch it."

"Are we still talking about the dog?" Holly asked with a grin.

"You two are incorrigible," Ivy said, feeling suddenly lighter than she had in days.

"You know it," Jolene said.

Ivy and Holly both laughed.

"Well, you may be scared of a little pile of fluff," Holly said as she waved a long-fingered hand toward the table laden with appetizers and drinks. "But I'm not missing out on that delicious spread. Plus, I need a glass of wine."

Jolene cast one more suspicious glance toward the dog, who had followed Isaac to a nearby table and now sat leaning against Isaac's leg, an expression of doggy contentment on his face.

When they reached the food, Jolene shook her finger at Holly. "I'd better not see you sneaking any food to the dog and encouraging him to hang around us while we're eating."

Grace stood near the end of the table, speaking quietly to a tall young man. The innkeeper turned to Jolene and said, "You should be fine. I think Winston has found his social companion for the evening."

"He's adorable," Ivy said.

Holly leaned into her arm and added, "And the dog is cute too."

Ivy felt her cheeks flame and hoped Grace knew that she hadn't intentionally had any part in that. She spoke more loudly than usual, hoping to plow right over Holly's embarrassing remark. "What kind of dog is Winston?"

"He's a mix," Grace said. "Shih tzu and mystery."

"I can see the shih tzu in those paws that look like dust mops," Holly said with a laugh. "My nana had a shih tzu, and I used to tease her that she adopted the dog just to keep the floor clean. Winston is big for a shih tzu."

"Yes, and every inch a charmer," Grace said.

Jolene sniffed.

Holly gave Jolene a poke. "I agree with Ivy. He's adorable."

But something in Holly's saucy smile made Ivy suspect her friend was referring to the young man again.

Ivy snuck a glance at the man. He'd pulled a notebook from his pocket and was staring at it morosely while patting Winston with one hand.

"I know that look," Jolene told Holly. "Remember why we're here, which doesn't involve attracting any strays. I'm sure he's a fine dog, but he can probably shed on command and my outfit won't be improved with dog hair."

"I think Winston is settled for the whole social hour," Grace said.

"Your outfit should be safe, but I'll keep an eye on him and head him off if he starts in your direction."

Ivy wondered if their hostess was growing annoyed at Jolene's negativity toward her sweet little dog.

"Let me introduce you to my son, Jake," Grace said, gesturing to the young man still standing beside her. "He's a software programmer, and he's visiting from Raleigh."

Jake greeted Ivy and her friends and asked them about their jobs.

"I'm a graphic artist in Charleston," Jolene said, then spoke for her friends. "Holly is a magazine editor in Atlanta, and Ivy works at an advertising firm in Charlotte."

They chatted with Jake for a few more minutes.

"I know that Holly has already met Isaac," Grace said. "But I don't think the rest of you have yet. Let's go say hello." She walked over to Isaac.

Ivy and her friends and Jake followed.

When the small group approached, Isaac stopped writing in his notebook and glanced up.

Winston wagged his tail at the newcomers, and Jolene stepped as far away from the dog as possible.

"Good evening," Grace said to Isaac, then made the introductions. Once the group began talking, Grace excused herself.

Holly bent to pet Winston. She laughed when the little dog wiggled with joy at the attention. "We'll let you get back to your work," Holly told Isaac. "We're going to get a bite to eat."

"It was nice meeting you," Isaac said to Ivy and Jolene.

Jake sat down next to Isaac, and they struck up a conversation.

As Ivy and her friends made a beeline for the food table, Jolene brushed at her clothes. "I'm sure I have dog hair all over me."

"No, you're fine," Ivy said, giving her friend the once-over.

"I've heard that you should never trust anyone who doesn't like dogs," Holly joked. "Don't forget that dogs are man's best friend."

"That saying should be about fish," Jolene said as she started filling her plate. "Now there's an ideal pet. They sit quietly in a tank and hardly make a mess."

Ivy was relieved the conversation had shifted to a safer topic. "Oh? Do you have fish now, Jolene?"

"Well, no," Jolene said. "But I had fish when I was a kid. I always loved them. They're so pretty. All the colors."

After Ivy and Holly loaded their plates, they followed Jolene to the farthest table from Winston.

"You know, Ives," Jolene said, reviving a nickname Ivy hadn't heard in years, "I may need to rethink my view on strays. It might be a good idea if you pick someone to have a light relationship with. It'll take your mind off what's-his-name."

Ivy's breath caught in her throat. She couldn't imagine anything she wanted to do less than that.

Jolene tapped the table next to Ivy's plate. "It would also help you recommit to the plan. Men are fun, but they aren't forever."

Ivy stifled a groan as she scrambled for a response. She honestly couldn't imagine what had ever made her go along with the plan in the first place. They'd all been so young and so sure that relationships were toxic by nature. They'd believed that the only way they could be happy and successful was to keep their dating lives light with no serious romantic entanglements.

Holly put her hand on Ivy's arm. "If you're up for a little romance, then there's a great possibility." She nodded toward Isaac. "He's quite gallant, and he's the strong, silent type. I appreciate that. It gives me more room to talk."

Ivy didn't know what to say, so she remained silent.

"On second thought, he might not be right for you," Holly continued. "You don't need the quiet type right now. If you went out with someone that quiet, you'd both just sit around and stare at each other."

"I'm not ready to jump back into a relationship," Ivy whispered, not trusting herself to speak any louder for fear of letting go and yelling at her friends. "Not now." *Not when my heart is broken.*

To her surprise, neither of her friends pushed the idea any further.

"Fine," Jolene said. "Then we'll go with my second favorite cure for heartache. Retail therapy."

"Excellent idea," Holly gushed. "I need some new dresses for all the Christmas events coming up." She lifted her purse from her lap and pulled out a flyer. "This talks about a play and musical events."

Ivy tuned Holly out as her friend read from the list. She'd seen the same flyer in her room, but she'd barely scanned it. She wasn't in an event mood, but she knew she'd have to take part in at least a few of them. There was no way Jolene and Holly would let her get away with hibernating in her room, no matter how luxurious it was.

Holly slapped the flyer on the table and pointed to one of the entries. "Of course, we'll have to rely on the clothes we brought with us for tonight."

"Tonight?" Ivy squeaked.

"Dinner and a comedy show at The Tidewater on the other side of the lake," Holly explained. "It's a fund-raiser of some sort. Grace popped in while we were chatting in your room to tell us to make reservations. Don't you remember?"

Ivy recalled being glad Grace's tap at the door had interrupted a story from Jolene about the man she was presently dating. Hearing about other people's relationships was not helpful. Ivy had paid little attention to what Grace actually said, but she was pretty sure she remembered politely declining the idea. "I do remember. And I also remember saying that I was probably going to have an early evening. I didn't call for a reservation."

"And that's exactly why we're here," Jolene insisted. "To keep you from curling up in a ball of misery instead of getting out and shaking off those blues." She smiled. "Luckily Holly and I called for reservations for the three of us."

Holly pulled out her phone and checked the time. "It begins in two hours."

"Two hours?" Ivy repeated, annoyed at the returning squeak in her voice. "I didn't pack anything to wear to a fund-raiser. Isn't that kind of thing usually fancy?"

"I asked Grace about it earlier," Holly said. "She said it wasn't. And we all look fabulous right now. I think we're fine."

Jolene tapped the table next to Ivy with one long nail. "But this only serves to prove that we're right. You need retail therapy, which we will definitely do tomorrow."

A slender blonde woman with dark-brown eyes stopped by the table to introduce herself. "Welcome to the Magnolia Harbor Inn. I'm Charlotte Wylde, Grace's sister and the other co-owner. We're excited that you're staying with us."

"I recognized you from the photo on your cookbooks," Holly said. "I have two of them and use them all the time. No one combines contemporary flavors with Southern classics as well as you do."

Charlotte's smile turned to one of open delight. "Thank you. I'm so glad you enjoy them." She extended her smile to include all of them at the table. "Are you ladies going to the fund-raiser at The Tidewater? It's for one of the owner's favorite charities, the children's wing of the local hospital."

"That's a great choice," Ivy remarked.

"We're going," Jolene said enthusiastically. "I love live shows, and some of us could use a night out." She gave Ivy a pointed look.

Ivy ignored her friend and remained silent.

"Will you be there?" Holly asked their hostess.

"Yes," Charlotte said. "I've been eagerly anticipating it for days."

"I have another question," Holly said. She still wore a slightly awed expression. "Do you have a suggestion of where we should go tomorrow to find cute outfits for the Christmas Eve party?"

"Miss Millie's in downtown Magnolia Harbor," Charlotte answered without hesitation. "The shop specializes in dresses, but you can get some lovely dressy pants and tops there as well."

"Your sister recommended it too," Jolene cut in, then grinned at Holly. "And it's near a bookstore."

"That sounds wonderful." Holly clutched Ivy's arm, clearly expecting her friend to join in her excitement.

Ivy tried to force her features into something resembling enthusiasm. She wasn't sorry she'd agreed to the comedy show and shopping, but she was beginning to suspect her Christmas was going to be a lot more stressful than she'd imagined.

So much for a quiet time of healing.

7

Isaac

Isaac glanced up at the sound of Holly, Ivy, and Jolene getting up to leave the veranda. The thought of sitting with the lively trio for an extended period was scarier than some of his harrowing experiences overseas, but he did envy their obvious closeness. Isaac couldn't think of anyone he felt that kind of bond with. It wasn't that he hadn't grown close to some of the soldiers he'd served with, but it was a different kind of connection, not the easy familiarity of the three friends.

With a jolt, Isaac realized that Holly was coming toward him. He hoped she didn't think he was staring at her. In a panic, he tried to come up with a valid reason for the attention, one that didn't make him sound creepy. But it was clear when Holly reached his table that she was neither angry nor offended.

She slipped into the chair near him and began rubbing Winston's ears. "Jolene is practically phobic about dogs," she said in a conspiratorial whisper. "But I couldn't leave without petting this little sweetie again. Grace said he's a shih tzu mix."

"I don't know much about dog breeds. Most of the kids in my neighborhood had mutts. But he is a nice dog." Isaac gave himself a mental kick for his lame babbling.

Holly motioned to the notepad on the table. "You've been busy. Can you share what you're working on? Your paper suggests it's been challenging."

Isaac contemplated the slightly rumpled notebook. The top page was covered in his scrawl, and nearly everything he'd written had been scratched out. "It's a speech. I'm going to visit an elementary school and talk to the kids tomorrow."

"Oh. Wow." Holly shuddered. "I can't imagine. Good luck with that."

Isaac almost told her how much her horror nearly mirrored his own—at least on the inside. Clearly Holly wore everything she thought on her face. He appreciated that quality. It must make her a terrible liar. Then he realized she was waiting for a response. "It's harder than I expected. I admit I'm a little nervous." *Talk about an understatement.*

"Why would you spend part of your holiday talking to kids? Why not go home? Or are you going home after you give your speech?" Then she laughed. "I'm sorry for being nosy. And I know I'm not one to talk since I'm away from home during Christmas too."

Isaac was surprised to find that he didn't mind Holly's questions. "I didn't want to go home. My mother passed away while I was still overseas, and now it's not the same there. You see, my dad died when I was a little kid, so it was Mom and me against the world for many years."

"She must have been proud of you," Holly said. "Serving your country."

"She was," he said hesitantly. "But my dad was killed in the service, and she worried about me." He shook his head. "Then it turned out to be the one of us not in the war zone who died." He took a deep breath that hitched slightly in his chest. "Sorry. I didn't mean to be so depressing."

"Loss isn't depressing," Holly said. "It's hard and painful and a part of being alive. And grief takes time." She reached out to pat his arm. "If you need a shoulder to cry on, let me know. And I can listen to you rehearse your speech if you want. I'm impressed that you'd talk to a roomful of kids. You're a brave man."

"Holly!" someone called from across the veranda. Holly's friend Jolene stood in the doorway, tapping a foot. "Come on. We have a show to attend."

"Gotta go. Can't keep the boss waiting." Holly laughed, gave Winston one last pat on the head, and rushed off.

Isaac watched her go. Holly sure was an interesting woman, but the most shocking part was that he felt a little better even though they'd spoken only briefly. He really had been isolating himself. But tomorrow that would change. The school visit would be his chance to connect with another caring and interesting woman, one he desperately wanted to meet, talk with, and pour out his feelings to. And maybe his life would change after that.

He picked up his pen and examined the scratched-out mess on the notepad. Isaac had always been a big believer in being prepared for a mission, but he wasn't sure there was any way to be totally prepared to talk to a group of fifth graders.

The sound of heels tapping drew his attention from the page again. Grace was clearly coming his way. She waved toward Winston, who had returned to leaning against Isaac's leg. "I hope Winston hasn't been a nuisance."

"Not a bit," Isaac assured her. "I used to have a scruffy little dog when I was a kid, and Winston is a nice reminder of Patch. He's been a comfort, considering this isn't going so well." He gave the notepad a nudge with the pen, pushing it slightly askew.

"Working on a letter?" she asked.

Isaac shook his head. "A speech. I'm talking to a bunch of kids tomorrow at the elementary school. I'm guessing you're familiar with it."

Grace nodded. "It's a wonderful school. My cousin Paisley Russell teaches there."

"She's the one who invited me," Isaac said.

"I should have known," she said with a smile. "It's nice of you to speak to the students. I'm sure they'll be thrilled."

"I hope so," he said, giving the notebook another push. "Actually, I mostly want to tell them how much I appreciate the letters they sent to me while I was overseas. I couldn't always answer them, so I wanted to come and say how much they mattered."

"The children will be glad to hear it," Grace said. "And I am so glad the letters were helpful. It was Paisley who started the program for the classes to write to soldiers. It's been a huge success, and I think most of the school participates now."

"It makes a difference," Isaac said. "The letters helped me through some dark times."

"Having you there is going to be a boost to the program," Grace continued. "The teachers don't do it for the thanks, of course. But it helps to know it makes a difference."

"I'm proof that it does," he said. "I'm not sure I'd be here without them."

They were both quiet following his confession. The silence was heavy with the truth of his words.

Isaac shifted nervously in his seat. He didn't usually admit his problems to people, and here he'd done it to two different women in the space of minutes. He pushed the thought aside and returned to the speech. "Do you have any tips for talking to a group of children? I'm honestly scared. I don't want to blow it."

"I'm sure you'll do a great job," Grace assured him. "Just remember what it was like to be a child when curiosity was one of the driving forces of your life. What would you have wanted to know? Imagine a young Isaac, and answer his questions with your speech."

Isaac winced. His mother had complained once that he was a fountain of questions as a child. He could ask questions about mud.

"You're making my head spin," his mother had told him. "I don't have all the answers. You're going to have to ask your teachers or read a book."

At the time, Isaac had thought his mother was being unreasonable, but now the idea of facing that kind of onslaught made his stomach clench with nerves. "I believe you just made me more scared than ever," he admitted.

"Oh, I'm sorry. That certainly wasn't my intention."

"It's okay. Maybe after I mull it over for a while, it'll be better. Thank you all the same."

Grace patted his shoulder. "I'll offer one more bit of advice. No matter how the speech goes over, try to keep in mind that by tomorrow night it'll all be over."

With a chuckle, Isaac said, "Thanks. Now that is comforting."

Ivy

When they joined the group standing outside The Tidewater, Ivy was glad to see that only a few people were dressed up for the comedy show. Ivy and her friends would blend in with the crowd. Then she glanced at Holly and Jolene and chuckled. On second thought, they would never blend in with a crowd.

"What's so funny?" Holly asked.

"I was thinking that you were right. Our clothes are fine." Ivy gave her friend a sideways hug. "You're always right."

Holly giggled. "Of course I am."

"And I'll remind you that my clothes and my style are more than fine," Jolene ran her hand down the long sweater she wore over leggings. Then she surveyed the area. "I'd say this is *the* place to be."

Ivy nodded as she scanned the crowd. "But it makes me worry for Charlotte. She hadn't left when we did, and I don't see her. I would hate it if she couldn't get in."

"She's from here," Jolene said, barely needing to raise her voice above her normal volume to be heard over the buzzing crowd. "I expect she knew how it would be. She's surely got a reservation. Remember, it was Charlotte's sister who told us we needed one."

"Of course. I'm being silly," Ivy said, but she continued to scan the crowd for Charlotte.

The greeter walked over to them and asked their names.

Ivy was relieved to find their reservation was on the list, but she couldn't set aside her concern for Charlotte. She knew it was a nervous tic she had. Once a worry got into her head, it was hard to get it out. "Do you know Charlotte Wylde?" she asked the greeter. "Can you watch for her? If she doesn't have a reservation, she could join us when she arrives. I wouldn't want her to be turned away."

The greeter's polite smile turned amused. "Miss Wylde has a seat waiting for her. You needn't worry."

"Told you," Jolene said as she linked an arm with Ivy. "You need to learn to relax, Ivy-vine."

"I'll try," Ivy acquiesced as the group headed for their table.

Their seats were rather far from the stage, but Ivy didn't mind. Instead, they were close to tall windows offering a view of a large patio area and the lake beyond it. Ivy gazed out the window, taken again by what a lovely area her friends had chosen for their Christmas reunion. She wished she was in a better emotional state to appreciate it.

"Well, I wish we could have had a table closer to the show," Jolene grumbled, echoing part of Ivy's thoughts. "I'm not sure it would be possible to get farther away without going outside."

"But the space is pretty intimate," Holly said. "There aren't any bad tables." Then she wrinkled her nose. "Except maybe the one by the bathrooms."

Ivy glanced in the direction of Holly's gaze and saw a laughing couple seated at the table Holly had referenced. They didn't appear to be upset about the location of their table. Ivy and Ballard used to be that way. It seemed that they could find a silver lining in any cloud. With a sigh, she wished she could find one now.

"Oh, stop sighing and look over there," Jolene whispered, nudging Ivy. "Isn't that Charlotte? And who do you suppose that handsome man is?"

Ivy followed Jolene's not-so-subtle pointing and spotted Charlotte walking into the room with a startlingly handsome man. He pulled

Charlotte's arm through his and led her away from the crowd with the pleased expression of a man who appreciated having a lovely woman on his arm.

"He reminds me of a movie star," Ivy said. "One of those men who's too gorgeous to be real."

"I would enjoy gazing at him across the table," Holly agreed. "Though he's a little short."

"You think so?" Jolene asked. "I don't mind shorter men myself."

Ivy tuned out her friends' chatter about what made men attractive. For a moment, she was glad neither of them had ever seen Ballard. They would have thought him ordinary in appearance, and Ivy supposed he was. Ballard was about the same height as Charlotte's friend, but he lacked the confidence the other man exuded, a confidence that came too close to arrogance for Ivy's taste. *Shame on me*, she scolded herself. *I'm sure Charlotte's friend is nice.* He had to be if Charlotte liked him. Both Charlotte and Grace struck her as kind, levelheaded women.

Holly's hand on Ivy's arm brought her back into the conversation. "Hey, you never showed us a picture of your ex."

Ivy blinked at Holly, amazed at how her friends kept acting as if they could read her mind. It was almost disquieting. "I don't have any," she said. Earlier when Ivy had deleted all Ballard's photos and everything else about him from her phone, it felt good. But now she had a sinking feeling, and she wondered if she'd made a mistake.

If Ivy had any pictures of Ballard, she still wouldn't show them to Holly and Jolene and let them pick apart his features. His pale eyes behind his glasses and his thinning hair would make him an easy target. Ivy couldn't bear to subject him to that, even if he'd never know.

"What does he look like?" Jolene asked.

"He's fairly average," Ivy replied. "Just an ordinary guy."

"Well, you deserve above average," Jolene said. "We all do. We aren't ordinary women."

Ballard wears his beauty on the inside, Ivy longed to say, but she knew that wouldn't be accepted by her friends. It was true that Ballard's unfaithfulness had broken Ivy's heart, but she refused to erase all the kind memories of him. She didn't know why he'd done what he had, but Ivy simply couldn't see him as a monster. *It must have been me. I wasn't good enough. I simply didn't deserve a man like him.*

Ivy turned her head away, hoping her friends wouldn't see how close she was to tears. She pretended to watch the audience with interest. Then her gaze swept across a group standing at the greeter's podium, and her feigned interest became sharply real.

Ballard?

Without another thought, Ivy hopped up from her chair and headed for the door. Behind her, Holly and Jolene called her name, but Ivy didn't stop.

The group of people with Ballard had been turned away, and they walked back out the front door as Ivy zigzagged around the tables. She assumed some extra tables had been added for the show, and the space between them was tight enough to make her passage slow. Her heart pounded in her chest as she murmured apologies for every chair she bumped into in her haste.

When Ivy arrived at the front, she headed straight out the door. Though the parking lot was decently lit, it still had plenty of shadows, and it was difficult to make out the faces of the few people who were outside. Ivy hurried down the steps and scanned the area, convinced that she would recognize Ballard no matter how much the shadows might try to hide him. Her heart would know.

Even though she searched the parking lot until her eyes blurred with unshed tears, she saw no sign of Ballard. She decided that she had imagined him. She had been thinking about him and missing him, causing her mind to turn some stranger into Ballard. That was the only logical explanation.

With a wry humorless twist of her lips, she realized that Ballard's average appearance would make it easier to see him in the faces of strangers. Hadn't that happened more than once before she'd left the city?

Ivy stood in the shadowy night until she'd calmed down enough to return to her friends. After she gathered her wits, she recognized there was no way Ballard was in Magnolia Harbor. He had no family in South Carolina and no business either. They'd talked enough that she was sure of that. And since he couldn't possibly have known Ivy was in Magnolia Harbor, he certainly wouldn't have come for her.

That man wasn't Ballard.

No way. No way at all.

9

Isaac

After a night filled with troubling dreams and far too much twisting and turning, Isaac gave his bed a guilty glance. He normally could be counted on to make his own bed, but this was probably beyond him. Especially with the different coverlets and pillows. How could anyone need so many pillows anyway?

With a determined effort, he turned his back on the unmade bed and went into the bathroom. He washed his face and stared into the mirror, realizing he'd studied his face more on this brief trip than at any other point in his recent memory. What was he searching for? And how could he possibly feel more unsettled this morning than he ever had when preparing for an overseas mission?

Isaac remembered Grace's advice from the night before and spoke aloud to the worried man in the mirror. "It'll be okay. They're just curious children."

At that thought, a parade of horrifying memories swept through his head, and he shook it as if to clear them out. "I hope they aren't too curious."

He walked back into the bedroom and grabbed his jacket from where he'd left it on a chair. Then he fished out the letter from the inside pocket and sank down into the chair to read it one more time. The encouraging words had gotten him through so much.

"'Everyone needs a little support now and then. You have ours always.'" As he read a couple of lines from the letter aloud, a familiar sense of calm came over him.

Isaac took a few deep breaths, reminding himself that she would be there during his speech. And she'd be rooting for him. He felt certain of that. *I'm not doing this alone.*

"Thanks again," he said. He stood and slipped the letter into the pocket of the jeans he was wearing. He'd change into his uniform before he left. He didn't want to risk the slightest chance of some of his breakfast marring the clean uniform.

Even though he wasn't feeling particularly hungry, he went down to breakfast anyway. One lesson from the military stuck with him: when there is food, eat it.

Surveying the spread in the inn's dining room, Isaac thought that it didn't hurt when the food was this appealing. A frittata loaded with a variety of vegetables and meat looked delicious, and the baskets of muffins gave off an aroma that reminded him of his mother's kitchen. He considered which foods would settle his stomach, then took a muffin and headed for the table.

Isaac had barely sat down before Holly slipped into the seat beside him with a full plate. He was surprised by how glad he was to see her, especially when he thought he had no interest in conversation with anyone this morning. He was too keyed up about the speech.

"That isn't much food for a man on a mission," she remarked, gesturing to his muffin.

"Probably not, but I think it's something the butterflies in my stomach will enjoy," Isaac said. "Did you have a good time at the comedy show last night?"

"Yes, it was great," Holly said. "You should have come. It would have taken your mind off your speech."

"I didn't want to go alone," he said. When he saw Holly about to speak up, he added, "And I didn't want to crash your party. Your reunion should be about the three of you, right?"

"You're right. And we did have a great time. I mean, Ivy got a little weird at the beginning of it and even went outside for a few minutes. I think she may have wanted to have a good cry. I wish she'd felt safe enough to have it around us, but Jolene can be a little insensitive."

Isaac blinked. He hadn't expected a flood of personal information about the sad-eyed woman he'd met the night before. "I'm sorry she's unhappy," he said, hoping it was an acceptable response.

Holly nodded, so what he said must have been all right. "She cheered up somewhat during the show. It was extremely funny. There were three comedians, all Southerners, which I appreciated as sometimes it seems comedians are laughing at us instead of with us. You know what I mean?" She didn't wait for him to answer before continuing. "Anyway, one comedian had a whole routine about how time works in the South, and I laughed until my stomach hurt." She proceeded to relay the joke, then giggled when she was done.

Isaac laughed along with her.

As Holly picked at her breakfast, she continued to share remembered bits from the show. Sometimes she led with the punchline, so Isaac had to reconstruct the joke in his head. But what amazed him the most about the conversation was the realization that he felt so much better. He guessed she was drowning his panic in words.

"What?" she asked, halting in the middle of a sentence. "You were laughing with your eyes, and I wasn't at a funny part."

"I'm not sure that's physically possible," Isaac said. "I mean, laughing with my eyes."

Holly waved off his comment. "Of course it is. I can always tell when someone's laughing at me in their head." She narrowed her eyes. "Were you laughing at me?"

"No, I wasn't." He held up both hands in surrender. "I was realizing that I felt better since you joined me."

Her eyes widened, and then she smiled radiantly. "I'm glad. You should feel good. It's almost Christmas. If you can't be happy at Christmas, when can you be happy?"

"That's a good point." Isaac poked at the remains of the muffin on his plate and sighed. "But I need to go change into my uniform, grab my stuff, and head out. I don't want to be late for the kids."

To Isaac's surprise, Holly leaned over and hugged him in a quick, companionable way. "You'll be great. I have faith in you."

"Th-thanks," he stammered, then fled the table with his cheeks burning. His confusion over that hug managed to keep the butterflies in his stomach napping through his run upstairs to his room to change and then all the way out to his car.

Once he was seated in his rather battered old Chevy, the butterflies seemed to wake up and flutter around in full force. He pressed a hand to his stomach. In a few hours, this speech would be over. He didn't know what was ahead, but no one was going to shoot at him.

"That's a plus," he said as he turned the key in the ignition and listened to the car come noisily to life.

As the car rumbled down the inn's driveway, Isaac practiced some opening lines in his head, but they all sounded ridiculous to him. He became even more nervous. Along with his nerves came the worst case of dry mouth he'd suffered in years.

"At this rate, I won't be able to talk by the time I get there." He decided to stop at a convenience store and buy a bottle of water and a pack of gum.

Of course, he'd spit the gum out before he got to school. It would hardly be appropriate for him to be chewing a wad of gum when he tried to speak. He remembered how much trouble he'd gotten into about gum in school when he was a kid. One of his teachers had made the kids caught with gum stand at the front of the class with the gum on their nose.

The memory brought an unexpected chuckle as he remembered how his cousin Lenny had started chewing gum every day after the new rule was put into place because he enjoyed standing at the front of the room and making faces at people. Lenny would have been great at that comedy night. He'd always made Isaac laugh when they were kids.

Isaac pulled the car into the parking lot, got out, and hurried into the convenience store. He considered a bottle of iced tea but ultimately rejected it. The tea was liable to make him jumpy, and he had no idea if it would be allowed in the classroom anyway. Instead, he snagged a bottle of water. Surely that would be fine.

"Excuse me."

Isaac jumped and spun around to see a tiny elderly woman peering up at him with a sweet look on her face. "Yes?"

"I wanted to say thank you for your service," the woman said. "Thank you so much."

Isaac nodded. "You're welcome, ma'am."

She smiled at him, then turned and ambled down the aisle.

Isaac grinned as he watched her go. He recalled all the people who had done the exact same thing since he'd come home. Then he thought of stories he'd heard about how some soldiers had received a far different welcome home years before.

He couldn't imagine how hard it would be to face what he'd seen overseas and then come home to an unwelcoming country. He definitely had a lot to be grateful for.

Isaac carried his purchases to the counter.

The cashier also thanked him for his service, though her tone was slightly less sincere, but Isaac appreciated the sentiment just the same.

As he walked back to the car, he unscrewed the top on the water bottle and swished the water around in his mouth before swallowing.

Climbing behind the wheel, Isaac realized the distraction inside the convenience store had calmed him down again. He turned the key in the ignition and was greeted with nothing more than a soft click. "Oh no," he mumbled and tried the key again. Still nothing.

He popped the hood latch and hopped out of the car. With one of the keys, he cleaned the connections to the battery. He'd left the car with Lenny before he'd been deployed because his cousin had promised to keep the car properly maintained in exchange for letting him use it. Apparently properly maintained hadn't meant the same thing to Lenny that it meant to Isaac. *Not so funny this time, Lenny.*

After doing all he could for the battery, Isaac got back into the car and held his breath as he turned the key. Again the soft click was all he heard. The engine wouldn't turn over.

With his hands resting heavily on top of the wheel, he scanned the parking lot. There was no one in sight. He couldn't believe that he was stranded in a strange town while the kids at school were waiting for him.

Isaac grabbed his phone and checked the GPS. He was only a couple of miles from the school, so if he didn't dawdle he had just enough time to walk there. So he climbed out of the car and retrieved his bag, then locked up and rushed out of the parking lot.

"I'm on my way, guys," he muttered. "I won't let you down."

10

Jake

In the first moments after Jake awoke, he squinted around the room in confusion, unsure of where he was. Then he woke enough for the memories to fall into place. He was in the Wisteria Loft Suite at the inn. The bed was better and bigger than the one in his apartment, and he'd slept well and deeply, despite the concerns on his mind.

He groped for his glasses on the bedside table. Then he grabbed his phone and groaned when he saw he'd missed breakfast. "Sorry, Mom," he said, though he knew his aunt would hardly let him go hungry. Raiding the fridge would give him more than enough food.

Jake patted the bed before standing. His own bed was only a full, and it rested on a simple metal bed frame. He hadn't seen the point of buying an expensive bed, but now he admired the antique wooden headboard on the king-size bed of the suite and had to admit the feeling of luxury was nice to wake up to.

It was difficult, but Jake resisted the urge to peek at his computer. He was supposed to be on vacation, so he intended to take a shower, get dressed, and have breakfast before spending a single minute online. His mom would be proud of him. Not that he was going to mention it to her, as that would involve admitting to her how many hours he spent online on a normal day. She would hardly let that go without comment.

After getting ready, he clattered down the stairs to the second floor, then took the back stairs to the kitchen.

Winston pawed at the bottom step, clearly having heard Jake's descent, and gave a single bark of welcome when Jake appeared.

"Good morning." Jake paused at the bottom to sit on the steps to pet Winston until the dog's excitement calmed.

"He's so glad to see you," Charlotte observed as she carried a mug of coffee over to Jake. "I'm guessing you could use some caffeine."

"Thank you." Jake accepted the mug and took a long sip. "It's really good."

"Since you missed breakfast, do you want me to whip you up some scrambled eggs?" Charlotte asked.

"With cheese?"

"You know it." She smiled. "And bacon."

"You are definitely the best aunt in the world," Jake said as he gave Winston one last pat and stood to follow Charlotte. He sat on one of the padded stools next to the kitchen island. "Anything I can do to help?"

"I would take that offer more seriously if you hadn't sat down before you made it," Charlotte said, her eyes bright with teasing.

"I can get back up." He started to rise, but his aunt waved him away as he'd expected.

His mom walked into the kitchen, and her pleasant expression bloomed into a wide smile. "Nice to see you up, sleepyhead. I considered sending Winston in search of you."

"I thought you wanted me to rest," Jake said.

"I do," Mom agreed. "Though I suspect your late start is mostly because you didn't go to bed at a reasonable hour. You could have gone to the comedy show instead of holing up in your room."

"I know," Jake said. "I'm sure the show was great."

"It was," Charlotte said as she cracked eggs into a bowl.

"I needed to work on a little bit of code for the new app," Jake said.

"What new app?" Charlotte asked. "I thought Gift Assistant came out recently."

"Yes, and it's already been so successful that we're working on a companion to it," Jake said. "We're hoping to release the new app right after the first of the year." He sighed deeply. "I wish we could have had it done for the holiday season, but it wasn't possible."

"And what important human interaction does this new app replace?" his mother asked, then put her hand to her mouth. "I'm sorry. I know your apps help people. I shouldn't have said that."

Jake hopped off his stood and gave his mom a hug. "Really, it's okay. I wasn't offended. I appreciate that you're old-school. It means I can always turn to you for balance."

Charlotte began whipping the eggs in the bowl with a small whisk. "I never heard exactly what Gift Assistant does."

"It's designed to help people think of presents for the difficult people on their gift-buying list," Jake explained. "It asks a series of questions about the person and gives suggestions on what to buy."

"I can imagine it now. What kind of gifts do they want?" Charlotte asked, dropping into a robotic tone.

"It's a little less obvious than that," Jake said as he walked over to the fridge for the pitcher of orange juice he knew would be in there. His mom loved orange juice, so there was no way they didn't have any.

"What do you mean?" Mom asked.

Jake poured a glass of orange juice and took a sip. "There are questions about what article of clothing you most associate with the person. What are their favorite topics of conversation? What color comes to mind when you think of the person?"

"Very interesting," Charlotte remarked as she grated cheese.

"The theory behind the app is that we know a lot more about people than we think we do," Jake said. "But when it's time to buy someone a gift, we can blank on what we know and panic. So the app quizzes you to help you sort out what you do know about the person. It's a lot more complicated than you imagine and based on tons of research into buying habits of the population as well as some psychological studies."

Charlotte nodded. "That does sound useful."

"It sounds complicated to me," his mom said. "Buying gifts should be a challenge. It makes you think deeply about the people around you." Then her expression turned guilty and apologetic. "I'm sounding critical and unsupportive again. I'm sorry. I know an app must be a lot of work to make."

"The research was, but the programming wasn't terrible," Jake said. "And I'm only hitting a few snags on the new app. I should have them untangled before I go back to work."

"Well, you need to work downstairs or go out and get some fresh air for a little while this morning," Mom said. "I have to start cleaning the suites as soon as the ladies head out for their shopping trip. Isaac already left."

Jake sat down with his glass of juice. "Honestly, you don't need to clean up after me. I know where the laundry room is. Besides, I've been taking care of myself just fine."

Mom shook a finger at him. "Don't you dare try to rob me of my chance to mother you." Then she grinned, belying the stern expression she'd been faking. "I'll be doing your room last because I want to poke around in some boxes on the third floor once I'm done cleaning. I'm sure I can find that ornament you mentioned."

"Please don't go to any trouble on my account to search for RoboGuy." Jake didn't put a lot of energy into his protest as he knew there was no point. His mom had found a mission, and she was going to stick with it until it was accomplished. In times like these, it was best to back off and let her get the job done.

Jake knew he'd gotten his tendency to live in his own head from Dad. His mom had told him more than once that his dad had been able to keep a secret for days while she tended to crack in hours. But Jake knew that his determination once he was on a task was purely from his mom. She'd never seen a challenge she couldn't overcome eventually. She'd met the challenge of being a single mom after his dad died. Jake had never known a moment when he didn't feel loved and supported.

Mom kissed Jake on the cheek. "Go outside. It's gorgeous out there today and warmer too. Take Winston. He gets too many treats so he can use the romp."

Jake knew he might as well surrender. "I'll do exactly that."

"Thank you." His mother sailed out of the kitchen with a satisfied smile on her face.

As soon as she was gone, Charlotte set a plate of scrambled eggs and bacon in front of him. "Are you going to tell your mom what's bothering you?"

During the banter with his mother, Jake had nearly forgotten anything was bothering him, but it rushed back with his aunt's words, making his cheeks warm. He didn't answer right away, bending over his plate to breathe in the aroma. "These eggs smell amazing," he said and shoveled a forkful of them into his mouth.

Charlotte folded her arms over her chest. "What does that mean? You're not going to answer my question, or you don't plan to tell your mom?"

Jake chewed and swallowed. "What makes you think something is bugging me?"

"Only knowing you for your entire life," Charlotte said.

Jake toyed with his eggs for a moment. "I'm fine. I really am. But if that changes, I'll be sure to let you know." He waited for his aunt to poke holes in what he'd said. It would be easy enough.

To his surprise, Charlotte seemed willing to let it go, at least for now. "So, I'm still deciding on the Christmas party menu," she said, changing the subject. "I'm considering a carrot, parsnip, and potato gratin or possibly a brussels sprout dish that's a bit of a stir-fry. I'm thinking of adding onions, red peppers, cranberries, cashews, and bacon to it. It'll be colorful and festive."

"I'll bet Paisley's kids will be thrilled with those options," Jake responded with a laugh. "You might ruin Christmas for them."

"Children benefit from having their palate challenged now and then," Charlotte argued.

"Sure they do. Why, that was my favorite thing as a child—wondering how my palate was going to be challenged that day." Jake shoved more eggs into his mouth as he listened to his aunt talk about flavor combinations. He was glad she'd stopped asking what was bothering him. He didn't make a habit of hiding things from his family, but he didn't want to ruin anyone's Christmas either, not until he was sure about his decision.

And if he made the choice that seemed the wisest, he was going to ruin the family Christmas more than parsnips or brussels sprouts ever could.

Isaac

By the time Isaac spotted the sign for Harbor Elementary School, a fine sheen of sweat lay on his skin, especially under his uniform. He felt generally rumpled, though he was relieved that he had made it in time for his speech. He covered the last yards at a trot.

When he'd left the inn, he still carried the hope that he'd get to the school early and have a chance to chat with the kids' teacher before the presentation. That seemed unlikely now.

"That'll be okay," he whispered. "We'll have time afterward."

Isaac reached the front door and pressed the visitor's button set in a panel cut into the brick facade.

In moments, a female voice asked, "How may I help you?"

"I'm Isaac Ryan. Paisley Russell is expecting me. I'm speaking to her fifth-grade class today."

"Welcome, Mr. Ryan," the woman's voice said. "You'll need to show your ID and sign in. The office is on your right."

Isaac heard a soft buzz and a click from the door. He opened it and walked inside. The door to the right had large glass windows on either side of it, and a tall woman with gray hair waved at him. He entered the office.

"Welcome." The woman thrust a clipboard at him. "I know the kids are eager to see you."

"Are you Ms. Russell?" Isaac asked as he took the clipboard. He couldn't match the worn look of the older woman in front of him with the letter in his pocket.

She introduced herself, but her name blew right through Isaac's head without registering. "I'm the school secretary." She went on without pausing and explained how Isaac could get to the classroom. "Paisley intended to send her teaching assistant down to welcome you, but there was a classroom catastrophe that tied them up."

"That's all right," he said as he signed, relief making his tone more cheerful than he felt. "I had my own snags this morning. I can handle the walk."

"Great. I need to see your ID, and then you'll be on your way."

Isaac removed his wallet from his pocket and showed her the identification.

The secretary raised her eyebrows. "You're from South Carolina. That's nice. At least you'll be able to make it home in time for Christmas."

Isaac didn't want to get into his holiday plans with a stranger, so he simply smiled.

When he exited the office, a young woman rushed down the hall toward him. She reminded Isaac of Holly's friend Jolene, though this woman had black hair and Jolene's hair was fiery red. Plus, the woman rushing at him seemed far too concerned, an expression he couldn't reconcile with Holly's confident friend.

"Are you Isaac Ryan?" the young woman asked breathlessly.

He nodded.

"I'm Paisley Russell's teaching assistant. I'm sorry I wasn't here to greet you. One of the children accidentally stabbed himself with a pencil, and it took several minutes to convince a few of the other students that he wouldn't have to go to the hospital for lead poisoning."

Isaac nearly laughed. He clearly remembered tripping and landing on a pencil stub at about that age and being certain he was going to get lead poisoning. "I hope the kid's okay."

"He'll be fine. He's down at the nurse's station. But I don't know how patient he'll be since he doesn't want to miss seeing you."

Her words reminded him that he was about to be the center of attention for a roomful of children, and the butterflies flapped furiously in his stomach. "I hope they aren't expecting too much."

The young woman smiled. "Actually they're pretty easy to please. You're a nice change of pace, and they'll be glad to meet the soldier they wrote to. Plus, it's almost Christmas so they're stirred up already. Don't worry. They'll be thrilled with you."

Isaac wasn't sure that knowing the kids were "stirred up" was comforting, but he merely nodded. He was glad that she filled the rest of the walk with chatter about the coming holiday.

Isaac surveyed the walls as they passed. Outside each classroom was a display made from projects created by the students. Isaac didn't remember his school being so colorful and full of interesting things to see, but he had a far different perspective then. He'd seen school mostly as an obstacle that kept him from doing more interesting things.

"Here we are," the teaching assistant announced as she opened a door and led Isaac into a large classroom.

As one, the kids craned their necks to stare at him, and some hopped out of their seats to get a better view.

Isaac was pleased to see every shade of skin tone seemed to be represented in the group with the one unifying feature being an excited smile on every face.

The teacher strode across the room and held out her hand. "Isaac," she said warmly, "I'm so glad you could come. I'm Paisley Russell."

Isaac shook her hand. It was cool to the touch and felt small in his. As he'd expected, Paisley was lovely. She was also older than his mental image of her, probably around forty, making her well older than Isaac. And he could hardly miss the wedding ring shining on her left hand.

Isaac forced his own smile, even as disappointment rumbled in his stomach. *I'm an idiot. Of course she's married. How could anyone so kind and wonderful not be married?* He'd tried not to admit, even to himself, how much he'd been hoping that he would find more than a pen pal here at the school, and now he was embarrassed at his own foolishness. Though thoroughly flustered, Isaac managed to stammer out his thanks to Paisley for inviting him.

If Paisley noticed his distress, she did an excellent job of pretending she didn't. Instead, she turned away and introduced Isaac to the class. "I know I can count on you to treat our guest respectfully and well. We all owe him a debt of gratitude for his service. Let's give a warm welcome to Mr. Ryan."

The class applauded enthusiastically.

Isaac discovered the smile he turned to them felt far easier on his face.

As soon as the clapping stopped, Isaac thanked them and quickly covered the things he was sure they already knew, including his rank and how long he'd been in the service. "The letters you sent to me were very special, and they mean a great deal." He pulled a sheet of paper out of his pocket and unfolded it. It held the notes he'd made for the speech. "When I was feeling incredibly lonely and far from home, someone wrote this for me. 'I told my baby sister that I was writing to a real soldier. She kicked her feet so I think she was excited. She also threw up a little, but I don't think that had anything to do with you. Babies throw up a lot.'"

The class laughed.

"I reacted just like that," Isaac said, "and the laughing helped me through that day."

A girl with thick glasses and a long braid hanging down her back raised her hand.

Isaac pointed at her. "Do you have a question?"

The girl's cheeks pinked, and she said, "I wrote that. My little sister doesn't throw up so much anymore. And she doesn't smell as bad either."

Isaac chuckled. "I'm glad to hear it."

"So is my mom," the little girl said, making Isaac laugh again.

He returned to his notes over and over, telling the kids about low points he'd suffered and reading lines from the letters that helped him through. Each time, a hand would shoot into the air and a child would claim the letter. Isaac was impressed that they remembered their own words so well. Clearly they'd been deeply invested in writing to him.

When Isaac had exhausted all the lines he'd copied onto the paper, he folded it back up and slipped it into his pocket. "There are more letters and more tough times, but I'd like to take a few minutes to answer your questions. I may not be able to answer everything, but I'll do what I can."

A sea of hands went up.

He picked a student from the front row, a boy who hadn't written one of the letters Isaac quoted.

"Were you scared a lot?" the boy asked.

Isaac nodded. "I think every soldier is scared, at least sometimes. Soldiers have to do some very hard, very scary things. It can be difficult to get through those times."

"Then why would anyone want to be a soldier?" the same boy asked without raising his hand, earning him a stern look from his teacher, one the child didn't seem to notice as his eyes were locked on Isaac.

"When I was not much older than you, I decided I wanted to live a life that mattered," Isaac said. "There are many different ways to do that, but being a soldier is the one I chose. It's also what my father and my grandfather chose. I guess you could say it's the family business. It felt right for me."

Another child asked a question, again without raising a hand. "But why is it a life that matters?"

"You know that police officers and firefighters help and protect people, right?" Isaac asked.

The kids nodded nearly in unison.

"The fire department brings a fire truck over every year," a little girl chimed in. "And we get to see all the stuff on it up close!"

"Fire trucks are cool," Isaac said. "And firefighters have to be really brave because fire is scary. But they do it, because protecting people is so important to them. Soldiers protect people too. But we have to do our jobs a long way from our families. None of us would do that if we didn't know it was important. We figure we go far away so our families back home will stay safe."

"What's your family like?" another girl asked.

"I don't have much family," Isaac replied. "But with all your letters, I think of you guys when I think about who I went there to protect. It helped me stay grounded. You helped me. I'll never stop being grateful for that. Thank you."

Taking a step forward to stand beside Isaac, Paisley cut in before another student could shout out a question or a remark. "I know you're all excited, but remember to raise your hands." She smiled at Isaac and took a step back again.

Several children raised their hands.

Most of the questions after that were less emotional. Isaac fielded questions about Army jeeps, his uniform, and how sand felt in a faraway country. The breadth of the questions reminded him of what Grace had said to him. These kids were curious about so many things.

By the time the last hand went down, Isaac felt positively exhausted. He backed away and leaned against one of the classroom walls.

Paisley thanked him and reminded the children to show their

appreciation, which resulted in enthusiastic clapping and one whistle. The whistler received a brief admonishment from the teacher.

As soon as Paisley had calmed the class, she walked to Isaac's side. "Now I want to extend a lunch invitation to you from the class," she said, speaking loud enough for the students to hear, which resulted in another round of cheering.

Isaac noticed this round was quickly suppressed by the teaching assistant.

"It's a bit of a potluck as the class brought in their favorite foods to share," Paisley told him in a quieter voice. "So if you're open to some adventure eating, we'd be so glad to have you join us."

"Thank you." He followed Paisley to a table laden with food. The lunch offerings varied from packaged cupcakes to empanadas stuffed with spicy meat.

The little girl with the long braid and glasses pointed to plantains stuffed with meat and peppers. "My grandma made those. They're my favorite."

"They look great," Isaac said as he took one of them. He finished filling his plate, then sat down at the other table.

After everyone else went through the buffet line, they joined him at the table.

Isaac was impressed with how well the kids ate the food. He'd been a picky eater at that age and wouldn't have touched anything more exotic than chicken nuggets, despite the scolding from his mother, who had seemed convinced he was going to get rickets or some other horrific condition. He turned to Paisley and said, "These kids are terrific."

"I think so," she said. "And they think the same of you. You're really special around here."

"You guys did a great job of making me feel special," Isaac said. Then he remembered that his car was sitting in a convenience store parking lot and set his plastic fork down on his empty paper plate. "Can you tell me the name of a good mechanic around here?"

"Oh no," Paisley said. "What happened?"

He explained his car's breakdown at the convenience store and the brisk walk to the school that followed it.

"You probably need a jump," Paisley said.

"I think that's it."

"Let me call my father. He'll drive you to your car and help you out." Paisley stood and picked up her plate and Isaac's. "I'll toss these and call him."

"I would hate to put your dad to that kind of trouble," Isaac said.

"It's no trouble. He loves helping. Let me make the call, and I'll be right back."

The kids took advantage of the time Paisley was away to drag Isaac around the room and show off different drawings and projects they'd done. He wasn't always sure of what he was seeing, since sometimes a few of the kids talked at once, but he found their cheerful eagerness to include him in their day buoyed his spirits. In fact, this was turning into the best day he'd had in a long time, even with his embarrassing realization of barely suppressed feelings for Paisley. At least he hadn't told anyone else about the silly romantic ideas he'd been carrying around.

Paisley joined the classroom tour before the kids could start a second lap around the room. "I think Mr. Ryan probably saw everything the first time," she said as she shooed the children back to their desks.

The children trudged to their seats and sat down.

"Did you get enough to eat?" Paisley asked, ushering Isaac over to the spread of food on the table. "There are some nice desserts."

"Maybe a cupcake," Isaac said, helping himself to one of the treats.

Once they were seated again, Paisley said, "You're staying at the Magnolia Harbor Inn, right? It belongs to my cousins."

Isaac nodded. "Grace told me that you started the soldier letter program. She's very nice."

"I think so too. And Charlotte cooks like a dream," Paisley said. "We'll be there for the Christmas Eve party, if you're staying that long. You'll be able to meet my husband, Bryson, and my kids. Sam is seven, and Monica is five. They can be a little rowdy, but I wouldn't trade them for the world."

"I'm surprised you didn't mention your family in your letters," Isaac said, hoping his tone didn't sound accusatory. It felt a little accusatory. He couldn't help but wonder how she could let him think she was single and that she could care about him.

"I never knew how much to talk about things like that," Paisley replied. "I would pray about what to put in the letters, what would be helpful in the moment. But I suspected that too much talk about my family might be more depressing than encouraging since you were so far away from your own loved ones."

Isaac realized that could possibly be a correct assessment. There were times when hearing about someone else's safe and happy life back home would not have made him feel better. But the kids wrote about that sort of thing, and it always cheered him. He stifled a sigh. Emotions were confusing and hard to predict. "You did a great job. I used to carry your letters around and read them whenever I felt down."

She smiled at him. "I'm glad."

Isaac took a bite of the cupcake so he didn't have to respond. He was relieved that he hadn't said something stupid to reveal how he'd talked himself into being half in love with a woman he'd never met. He still appreciated what Paisley had done for him. The words in her letters were no less insightful because his dream of her being the one for him had turned out to be a fairy tale.

But he was embarrassed, and he thought it might be best if he went home to Georgia and skipped out on the Christmas Eve party. If anyone at the inn figured out how he'd felt about Paisley, he would be horrified.

Yeah, it'll be better for everyone if I go home.

So why did the thought make him feel even more miserable?

12

Ivy

Main Street in downtown Magnolia Harbor was busy. Shoppers still hunting for last-minute Christmas gifts tended to have less selection but stronger motivation. Ivy was impressed that no one had resorted to shoving to get into shops.

A harried woman bumped into her, sloshing coffee from a cup in her hand. It barely missed splashing Ivy's arm, but it probably wouldn't have stained anyway. Ivy's yoga jacket in a neat blue check was cozy against the cooling breeze and resisted most of the spills she'd had with it on. When she'd packed it, she worried it was a little too casual for such an incredibly posh inn, but it was fine for the shopping outing.

"I think he's adorable," Holly said, raising her voice to be heard over a man playing a guitar and singing a Christmas song. As a result, her words cut through Ivy's distraction. "And he's sweet too."

Ivy wasn't sure who Holly was talking about. Then she remembered how much Holly had tried to combat Jolene's dislike of the inn's dog. Her friend was probably trying to defend the friendly creature again. "I think he's cute too," Ivy said supportively. "And well-behaved."

"What?" Holly said.

"Well, he never begged from a single plate that I saw." As she spoke, Ivy saw confusion change to amusement on the faces of both her friends.

Holly burst into laughter. "I'm sure Isaac would be glad no one saw him begging," she said through her giggles.

Despite the cool air, Ivy suddenly felt as if her face would ignite.

She put a cool hand against the heat in one cheek. "Okay, I admit it. I wasn't listening properly. I thought you were talking about Winston."

Jolene suppressed her own laughter to say, "Puppies, men—they're all the same. They can be cute and appealing, but they always come with more work than you expect."

Holly gave Jolene a friendly push. "You talk as if you never date, but you've dated more guys than I have."

"Yeah, well, I said they can be cute and appealing," Jolene admitted, her eyes dancing with mischief. "But that soldier you keep admiring is way too much work. He hardly says a word. You'd have to provide all the conversation, and you never know what's going on inside a silent man. I think I'll pass."

"That's probably wise," Ivy said. She tried to imagine the shy soldier trying to deal with Jolene and nearly laughed. He'd probably find it more terrifying than combat.

"Isaac's more open when you're alone with him." Holly's tone was casual, but Ivy suspected there was more going on behind Holly's chatter.

Apparently Jolene thought so as well. "So you're holding out on us. How many times have you been alone with him?"

Holly folded her arms over her chest and frowned. "If you're going to be that way, I'm not telling you anything."

"You're welcome to him. And I know you can talk enough for both of you. Not Ivy. If she and Isaac were alone, they'd just stare into their own laps like naughty children sitting in the corner."

"I'm not that bad," Ivy protested, wishing the conversation hadn't come back to her. "But I would never try to cut in on Holly's guy."

"He's not my guy," Holly insisted. "But I think we could be friends. And I think we'd both enjoy it."

"Good plan," Jolene said. "I wouldn't mind a quick holiday friendship. Especially the kind of friendship that comes with kissing.

Now that I think about it, Jake is kind of cute. I should ask him out. Since we won't be here long, it would be great. Just someone to hang out with."

"I don't know," Holly said. "I think he's got heavy things on his mind." Jolene stuck out her lip in a pout. "Now you're trying to ruin my fun."

As Holly and Jolene debated whether Jake was in the midst of some kind of inner turmoil, Ivy wondered if she really had anything in common with the two women in front of her. She used to think all the talk about keeping relationships superficial was amusing, but now it made her heart hurt.

Luckily they finally reached the dress shop they'd been seeking, and Ivy interrupted the debate to point it out.

They stopped to regard the window display at Miss Millie's. Most of the outfits were dresses, but Ivy admired the pretty gray pants matched with an asymmetrical navy blouse. The top had a touch of sparkle without being overly attention-grabbing. She mentioned how much she liked it to her friends.

"Not enough bling," Jolene announced.

"I prefer to go for understated," Ivy said.

Jolene opened the door and sailed through. "We'll see."

Ivy followed her inside, wondering if a feeling of impending doom was the right emotion for clothes shopping.

The store was decorated for the holidays with silver garland and clear lights wrapped around a few posts inside. Glittery snowflakes hung from the ceiling high enough to avoid even the tallest shopper. Many of the outfits on the mannequins inside reflected the festive shimmer a shopper would expect at this time of year.

Ivy was pleased to see the pieces of the outfit in her size. She could wear it to any of the dressier events and still make use of it for business functions as well. Though Ivy made decent money at the advertising firm where she worked, she had never been extravagant in her spending.

Her mother had taught her to choose good quality because they would both fit and wear better. "And remember, classic designs are always a good choice," her mother had said. "There's a reason why they're called classics."

Ivy smiled at the memory of her mother's advice and carried the clothes toward the changing rooms. Jolene and Holly were flipping through dresses, and Ivy merely waved at them as she went by. She didn't need any more dresses. She'd splurged on a few when she was dating Ballard, and now the sight of the rack where her friends stood made her sad.

"Don't dress for men," her mom had advised. "Dress for yourself, and you'll feel confident and happy. And if a man doesn't appreciate it, then you don't need him."

Ivy opened the dressing room door, glad for the chance to duck in before tears filled her eyes. Ballard had admired her taste in clothes and complimented her often. *And I do need him.*

Once she got her emotions under control, she slipped into the outfit. It fit her as if it had been tailored, and she found the sight of herself in the mirror cheering. She was definitely buying the outfit, even though she hadn't checked the price tag yet.

"One more splurge just for me," she whispered under her breath, then yelped as someone pounded on the dressing room door.

"Come out and show us," Jolene said. "It can't take that long to change your clothes."

Ivy opened the door. "You nearly gave me a heart attack."

"Think of it as your cardio for the day," Jolene said brightly, then looked Ivy up and down. "I was wrong about that outfit. You were right. It's perfect for you."

"Wow, Jolene Bettleman admitted she was wrong," Holly said, her voice full of mock wonder. "Would you be willing to say that again? I want to record it on my phone. I need to play it back a few times."

"I admit when I'm wrong," Jolene said. "I'm simply not wrong very often."

Holly chuckled, then turned her attention to Ivy. "That outfit is lovely on you. You should buy it."

"I'm planning to," Ivy said. "Did you two find anything?"

"A bunch," Jolene enthused. "I hung them in the next dressing room. I'll do a fashion show for you both."

"Sounds good," Ivy said.

"And I found something for you," Jolene added, holding a dress up to Ivy. "It's the exact same shade of periwinkle as your eyes."

"It's lovely, but I don't need a dress," Ivy said.

"Just try it on," Jolene insisted.

Ivy accepted the dress, then closed the door on her friends. She had to admit that the dress was pretty and fit her well.

When she opened the door, her friends gasped.

"It's gorgeous," Holly said.

"You have to buy it," Jolene told her.

"You know, I think I will," Ivy said. She closed the door again to change back into her previous outfit of jeans with a short-sleeved silk blouse and her yoga jacket. She had a rueful thought about spending so much money on clothes, but she couldn't pass up the two outfits. They seemed to be made for her.

As she got dressed, she heard Jolene and Holly chatting with each other from the dressing rooms on either side. Ivy picked up the beautiful clothes and carried them to the register. She'd watch while her friends gave their fashion show and referee as they argued about which one had picked the best dress. She remembered that about shopping trips with Jolene and Holly in the past.

The woman behind the small counter carefully folded the new outfits, wrapping each piece in tissue before slipping it into a shopping bag. "These are wonderful choices. They'll work well with your coloring."

"I thought so," Ivy said. She only winced a little as the woman told her the total price. *I'll go on a buying diet right after I get home*, she promised herself as she swiped her credit card.

With the large shopping bag in hand, Ivy glanced toward the dressing rooms. The doors were still closed, and she could hear her friends talking.

While Ivy waited, she drifted over to the shopwindow to admire the charming town. It had a different vibe than Charlotte, and no one would mistake Magnolia Harbor for the big city, despite the bustle of shoppers. Even so, Ivy loved it. She was glad her friends had chosen this area for their reunion, and she knew she could enjoy time spent here, if only her heart didn't ache.

Then Ivy glimpsed a man on the other side of the street. He was walking close to the shops, and a steady stream of people passed between Ivy and him. His profile had been as familiar as Ivy's own face, and the way the man moved rang a bell as well.

Ballard?

Ivy stepped even closer to the window, straining for another peek. She didn't see him.

Don't be ridiculous, she chided herself. *Ballard is in Charlotte. That's definitely not him.*

"Ivy!" Jolene shouted.

Ivy jumped and almost shrieked. As she turned, she saw a slight grimace pass over the face of the woman behind the counter. Ivy suspected Jolene was going to wear out her welcome here unless she bought a lot of clothes.

Ivy hurried across the shop to where Jolene stood outside the dressing room in a formfitting emerald-green dress that made her red hair blaze in contrast. What the dress lacked in sparkle, it made up for in the way the fabric seemed to flow over Jolene's curves.

"You probably shouldn't be shouting in here," Ivy whispered.

Jolene gave her a shocked look. "I wasn't shouting."

"She probably actually believes that," Holly chimed in as she stepped out of her dressing room. She wore a cool blue-gray cocktail dress. A scalloped-edge neckline featured a lace overlay, and small beading accents added a subtle holiday sparkle.

"You're both beautiful," Ivy said.

Jolene gave Holly a critical once-over. "Your dress is great. But mine is the most eye-catching."

Holly slung an arm around Jolene. "If you wore a burlap bag, you'd be the most eye-catching of the three of us. It's genetic."

Jolene beamed.

"Okay," Holly said, "I'm going to buy this dress, and I don't want to check out any others. I need to get to the bookstore."

"You and books," Jolene said, rolling her eyes. "You should have become a librarian instead of a magazine editor."

"I find enough time for both." Holly linked an arm through Ivy's. "What about it? Want to browse in the bookstore?"

"Hey," Jolene chimed in, "I'm not done trying on dresses."

"And you won't be until you try on every dress in the store," Holly said. "As soon as you do, you'll insist you need food to sustain you after all that work. Then I'll never get to the bookstore."

"I wouldn't do that," Jolene protested.

"Actually you would," Ivy said.

"And you have," Holly added.

Jolene threw her hands into the air. "Fine. I'll try on a couple of dresses on my own. You two go to the boring bookstore. Come back here when you're done, and we'll all go find some lunch."

"Great idea," Holly said dryly. "I wish I'd thought of it."

Ivy had to suppress a giggle. Holly certainly knew Jolene, and she was much better than Ivy at standing up to her. Ivy could take a lesson from Holly in dealing with Jolene—and life in general. Ivy was suddenly glad for being here with the two of them. They may not have a lot in common anymore, but there was still a connectedness built of knowing each other so well.

While Holly paid for her dress, Ivy waited at the window near the door, searching the sidewalks again, even though she was certain her mind was playing tricks on her. Ballard was similar in appearance to many other guys. He had that kind of face.

It's only my obsessing over him that's making me see him everywhere.

When Holly joined her, she nodded toward the window. "I love watching people. I do it all the time in Atlanta, but there are a lot more people. Here you could pick a spot and feel as if the whole town will walk by if you wait long enough."

Ivy had shucked off her yoga jacket while waiting for her friends and not put it back on in the warm store. But she regretted the decision as soon as they walked out into the cool breeze.

Holly noticed Ivy shiver and asked, "Did a goose walk over your grave?"

"What?"

Holly laughed. "That's something my grandmother used to say whenever she saw me shiver. I always thought it was silly. Why would there be a goose in a cemetery? I've walked through a few and never once saw a goose."

Ivy wasn't sure how to respond, so she simply put on her jacket again.

Holly didn't seem to mind Ivy's silence as she waxed on about the birds she'd seen in cemeteries.

While Holly talked, Ivy wondered again about having imagined she'd seen Ballard twice now. Was she on the verge of a breakdown? Or maybe there was something she was supposed to realize. Perhaps she had unfinished business with Ballard, and she needed closure. She could ask him exactly why he'd taken another woman to their favorite restaurant.

When they reached the door to the bookstore, Holly froze and pointed at the large glass front window. "Look at all those new releases. I can't wait to see what else they have inside."

And with that, Ivy let her friend drag her into the bookstore and out of her troubled thoughts.

13

Charlotte

Charlotte stood several feet away from the kitchen island, sipping a mug of coffee and studying her shopping list. She was a trained chef, with a cookbook collection that her publisher assured her was selling well. She also had been doing all the meal planning and cooking at the inn, including holidays, for years now. It made zero sense that she was having trouble choosing the vegetable dish for the Christmas Eve dinner.

"Dean wouldn't have this much trouble," she muttered. "He'd settle on something and charge ahead, even if it was a terrible idea. In fact, he'd never know if it was a terrible idea. He'd just barrel through."

And there was the problem. What if all her ideas for innovating the holiday menu were terrible? Realistically, she knew they wouldn't be, but they could be unwelcome. After all, the guest list included Paisley's children, who were more adventurous eaters than most, but they were still children. And her cousin Maria's children would be attending as well. Ricky and Sarah were older, but teenagers could be picky too.

"All I need is a plan," Charlotte mumbled.

"Why are you eyeing the counter as if it wants to bite you?" Grace asked as she walked into the kitchen. Her eyes widened. "Please don't tell me we have mice."

"It's okay. No mice." Charlotte spoke up quickly to ease her sister's panic. After all, it wasn't outside the realm of possibility that they could get mice, and this was the time of year that mice often slipped into homes, searching for a warm spot to stay for the winter. It never got bitterly cold in Magnolia Harbor, but it grew cold enough for mice and sometimes bugs to hunt for warmer spots indoors. "I'm still working on the party menu."

"And you think better by glaring at innocent countertops?" Grace asked.

"Sometimes." Charlotte sighed deeply. "I'll get there. How goes the cleaning? I could have helped." She noticed Grace had changed clothes since she saw her last. The vertical navy stripes on the off-white blazer reminded Charlotte of classic pillow ticking. Underneath it Grace wore a navy T-shirt that matched her jeans perfectly. "Have I seen that jacket before? I like it."

"I picked it up the last time I went shopping with Winnie. It reminded me of the striped pillows Grandma used to have. Do you remember?"

"That's actually what I was thinking. So are you all done upstairs? You didn't answer my question earlier."

"Because you followed it up with clothes talk." Grace went to the counter and poured herself a mug of coffee. She smiled at Charlotte. "My work upstairs was good."

Charlotte set her own mug on the counter and crossed her arms over her chest. "Okay, spill it. What has you so pleased?"

Grace's smile grew wider. "It's a secret. And you'll have to wait until Christmas to learn what it is."

Charlotte groaned. "This time of year is hard on anyone who suffers from acute curiosity."

"I imagine so." Grace took a long sip of her coffee, then gestured toward the notepad on the counter. "I also found an ornament Jake asked me about and hung it on the tree, so my whole day has been successful. I'm now ready to help you. That is, if you need any help with your menu dilemma."

"I need inspiration," Charlotte answered. "And a plan. I know everyone expects certain things from Christmas dinner."

"Like the family stuffing recipe."

"Yes, like that. I promise not to mess with the family stuffing recipe, but I do want to inject some newness into the menu. I want every meal I serve, every social hour I cook for to be definitely me. Tasty and nutritious but also unique."

"And they always are," Grace assured her.

"Thank you. But as Jake reminded me, we're going to have children at the party. I had been considering a carrot, parsnip, and potato gratin or possibly a brussels sprout dish, but Jake accused me of ruining Christmas for the kids." She held up her hand when Grace opened her mouth to defend Jake. "He wasn't rude, but it was a little deflating. I realized I should keep the tastes of the children in mind. They count too."

"I'm not sure Sam and Monica are the only ones who don't enjoy brussels sprouts," Grace said. "As I remember, Gus isn't the most adventurous eater either."

Charlotte dropped onto one of the stools, remembering their uncle's holiday favorites. "If I have to serve a green bean casserole, I'm not sure I'll survive."

Grace laughed. "I'm sure you don't have to make green bean casserole. Surely there is something between that and brussels sprouts that you could choose."

"You'd think so, but I'm not sure." Charlotte rested her chin on her hand and stared glumly at her shopping list.

"I thought I'd find you two in here," Winnie said as she breezed into the kitchen. "It's amazing outside. I hope you're going to go out there today." Their slender aunt wore a casual cotton jacket that was dressed up by lace cuffs. Elastic in the waist of the jacket offered a nice silhouette, and it even had pockets. Winnie was a big fan of pockets.

Charlotte got off the stool to walk over and hug her aunt. "I sort of have to, considering I don't live here."

"The short walk to your cottage doesn't count," Winnie said. "You should go for a real walk. I find it clears my head, and it's especially enjoyable when the day is cool enough to walk without sweating. All summer long, I count the days until this time of year when I can wear a jacket and feel cozy instead of sweltering."

"Speaking of the weather," Grace said, walking to the fridge but not opening it, "would you like some iced tea? Or does the cooler air mean you'd rather have a warm beverage?"

"I'd love a tall glass of sweet tea," Winnie said wistfully. "But I believe I'll have coffee with cream."

Winnie was diabetic and careful about her diet, but Charlotte knew she had a sweet tooth. Still, Winnie rarely complained about it or anything else. Like Grace, Winnie tended to search for the bright side of every moment. The two of them helped Charlotte overcome her sullen moments, even if only because Charlotte felt guilty about them around such upbeat women.

"I thought you'd be deep in holiday prep at your house," Grace said as she poured Winnie a cup of coffee.

"I was, but I didn't want to miss out on a walk," Winnie said. "I have to skip them too often in the summer heat." She took the coffee mug from Grace and murmured, "Thank you."

"When do you expect Maria and her family to arrive?" Charlotte asked.

"Sometime this afternoon," Winnie said. "And I want everything to be perfect for them."

"I'm sorry that Amelia and Harper can't make it for Christmas,"

Grace said. "It would have been nice to see all the cousins and their kids."

Winnie and Gus had four grown daughters—Amelia, Harper, Maria, and Paisley. Only Paisley lived in Magnolia Harbor. The others were scattered in different states.

"I wish they could all join us too. Hopefully they'll be able to next year." Winnie smiled. "It's going to be nice having children in the house on Christmas morning."

Charlotte chuckled. "You'd best not let Maria's kids hear you call them children. Ricky is fifteen, and I wouldn't be surprised if he's taller than his dad. And Sarah is thirteen. From my experience with teenagers, they don't enjoy being thought of as children."

"Your experience with teenagers?" Grace asked sweetly.

Charlotte wrinkled her nose at her sister, the closest she would dare come to making a face at Grace in front of their aunt. Charlotte had never been married. She had no idea if children would ever be in her future, though she often contemplated the idea of having a family. Sometimes it sounded wonderful. Sometimes terrifying. Still, she did have an edge on Winnie and Grace. "Fine, I remember how I used to be livid whenever a relative called me a child when I was thirteen."

Grace laughed. "As I remember, you were livid a lot at thirteen."

"Of course you remember it that way," Charlotte said as she settled back on her stool. "You were already grown with a brand-new baby when I was a teenager. You probably thought I was a spoiled brat."

Grace offered her a fond smile. "Actually, you were the best sister I could have ever imagined."

"Sure I was," Charlotte said.

"You were both good girls," Winnie said before changing the subject. "Tell me about your new guests."

"They're all lovely," Grace said.

"The three women are a little rowdy," Charlotte added.

"Maybe two of them," Grace admitted. "But Ivy seems quiet. The soldier in the Buttercup Suite is too. And I think they're both troubled."

Charlotte observed her sister with interest. Grace had mentioned her concerns about the guests before, but Charlotte still couldn't see it. She'd noticed Isaac and Ivy were quieter, of course, but she wondered at her sister's ability to tell when people were hurting. Charlotte had sensed something off about Jake, but even she wouldn't necessarily have characterized it as *troubled*. She assumed that Grace didn't seem to see it because she didn't want to.

"I know Isaac was a little worried about his presentation," Charlotte said. "But many people have a fear of public speaking and performance."

"I believe it's deeper than that," Grace said. "He was worried about his presentation, but I think he's grappling with something bigger. The same with Ivy. Though I think there is a lot of sadness mixed into whatever is troubling her."

"Maybe someone close to her died," Charlotte suggested. "Holidays are tough on grief."

"That is true," Grace said softly.

Charlotte flinched. She hadn't meant to bring up bad memories for Grace. Charlotte knew her sister had reconciled long ago to the loss of her husband in a train accident, but she didn't know if someone ever really got over something like that. She still mourned for her parents, but time had softened it to bittersweet memories in which love tempered the pain.

"You said Ivy was part of a larger group?" Winnie asked.

"There are three of them," Grace said. "Ivy, Jolene, and Holly. They were college friends, and this is a reunion for them. Ivy lives in Charlotte, Holly's in Atlanta, and Jolene is in Charleston. I suppose Magnolia Harbor was something of a middle spot."

"And the soldier?" Winnie asked.

Charlotte wondered what had prompted her aunt's interest. Winnie loved interacting with the guests at the inn and often helped out with inn functions, but she wasn't prone to gossip.

"Isaac is from Georgia too," Grace said. "I can't remember the name of the town offhand."

"Do you know what he did in the military?" Winnie asked. "His specialization? I assume soldiers do specialize these days." She sighed. "I'm afraid I don't know much about modern military life."

"You should come to the social hour tonight," Grace said. "You could ask him about it. I'd love to see someone get him out of his shell. I think Holly is trying. The two seem to have hit it off."

"Perhaps I will if I can squeak out the time." Winnie sipped her coffee with a thoughtful expression on her face. "Though with Maria, Adam, and the children—I mean, teenagers—arriving soon, I suspect I'll be tied up."

"What's with all the interest in the guests?" Charlotte asked, unable to hold back the question any longer.

Winnie raised her eyebrows as if the query surprised her. "Curiosity, I suppose. They sound fascinating."

Before Charlotte could probe further, Jake came down the back stairs and trotted into the kitchen. He hugged Winnie. "I knew I heard your voice down here. And for the record, I think I'm the most fascinating guest at the inn at the moment."

Winnie studied Jake's face intently. Then she smiled and said, "I think you might be right."

Isaac

Isaac chose one of the closest spots in the inn's small parking lot, one within jumper cable distance of a couple other cars in case he needed help getting his old Chevy to start again.

After Paisley's father, Gus Bennett, had jumped Isaac's car, he'd given him the name and address of the closest auto supply store. Isaac had come straight back to the inn after buying a few supplies. He needed some time to himself after the school presentation. Not that it had gone poorly. The kids were fantastic. But the revelations Isaac had to face were painful, and now he felt like an idiot. How could he have let himself fall for a woman who didn't exist, someone he'd made up in his head?

He trudged to the inn, barely noticing the beauty around him. Nothing even nudged his bubble of misery until he stepped inside and Winston rushed to greet him, a ball of bouncing fluff. Only the clicking nails on the marble proved Winston was a real dog and not a particularly cute child's toy. The dog's wild joy at seeing him lightened Isaac's heart a fraction, and he knelt down to ruffle Winston's ears. As he did so, he thought of the videos he'd seen online where veterans returned home to the boundless happiness of pets.

"I don't even have that," Isaac grumbled. The only thing that had greeted him when he got home was a car that had already failed him.

Isaac shook his head in an attempt to clear out the barrage of self-pity. He gave Winston one last pat and stood. For a moment, he turned toward the winding staircase, but he hated the thought of facing his empty room with nothing for company but his own lonely thoughts.

"Hey, Winston, you want to sit out on the veranda with me for a while?"

If Winston's dance around Isaac's feet was any indication, the dog thought the idea was great.

Isaac smiled as he headed through the house with the dog sometimes at his heels and sometimes racing ahead.

When Isaac reached the back veranda, he sank into a chair and drank in the view of the lake before him. Afternoon light played on the water, casting gold across the lake.

Winston stood on his back legs, putting his front paws on Isaac's knee.

"You want to sit with me?"

Winston wiggled so hard that he nearly fell over.

Isaac lifted the dog into his lap and stroked his fur. "You don't care if I'm a dope, do you?"

Winston gazed up at him with unfettered adoration.

Isaac laughed. "I'm not sure I'm worthy of that look."

"Winston is a great judge of character."

Isaac turned slightly to see Grace walking out onto the veranda. "He's a friendly little guy," he said. "I can't imagine how any of you could be blue with Winston around."

"We manage sometimes," Grace said. "Can I get you anything? I have a pitcher of sweet tea in the fridge, or I could bring out coffee."

"I wouldn't mind a glass of sweet tea."

A few minutes later, Grace brought out the tea for him and a mug of coffee for herself. She gestured to a chair close to Isaac. "Mind if I join you for a minute? I could use some time off my feet."

"Of course."

"How did your presentation go?" she asked.

"The kids were terrific, and Paisley's incredibly nice," he replied. "I owe her and her class a lot."

"I'm sure they were blessed to have you there as well." Grace took a sip of her coffee and studied him. "You don't appear as happy or relieved as I expected. Did you not do as well as you'd hoped? I'm sure the children appreciated you, no matter what you're thinking now."

"The talk was great, but the experience wasn't without its challenging spots," Isaac admitted. "For one, my car wouldn't start, so I had to walk part of the way to the school."

"Oh no. You should have called the inn. I would have given you a ride."

"That's okay," he said. "It wasn't very far. I've run a lot farther with a pack on my back. I wasn't even late when I got there."

"But something is bothering you," Grace said.

Isaac contemplated Grace's kind face, but he couldn't tell her how he felt. He could barely admit to himself that he'd completely imagined a relationship with a stranger, talking himself into the idea that Paisley was going to be more than a supportive voice in a letter. How could he say any of that to Grace when the woman he'd been mooning over was her cousin?

So instead he slipped into a slightly easier topic. "I'm trying to decide if I should stay here through Christmas. Now that my presentation is over, I could go back to Georgia."

Grace lowered her mug of coffee, though she still held it wrapped in both hands. "I can understand that. Do you have family there?"

"My cousin and his wife are there," Isaac said. "But we haven't been really close since I joined the service. I suppose I could crash their Christmas, but I'm not sure how thrilled they'd be."

"You're more than welcome here," she said. "There are a number of enjoyable events in Magnolia Harbor, and I think you would have a good time. We'll accommodate you in whatever you decide to do."

"Thank you," Isaac said. At least Grace didn't seem mad at him for suggesting he was thinking about leaving, despite having booked the room through Christmas. "I'll let you know."

"That sounds fine. I'd better get back to it. Let me know if you need anything." She reached over to scratch behind Winston's ears, then got up and walked inside.

As Isaac gazed out at the lake, he sank back in the chair, finally relaxing from his usual military posture. He'd stood strong for so long. Maybe it would be nice to relax for a few days. He could probably use a peaceful place to decide what to do with his life.

When Isaac heard conversation coming from inside, he was still petting Winston, who had fallen asleep in his lap and was snoring. Isaac strained to hear and picked out the sound of Holly and her friends. He hoped they weren't all coming out onto the veranda to break in on his quiet time. The voices began to sound farther away, and Isaac assumed the women had gone upstairs. *I'm safe until the social hour.*

"Isaac!"

He actually jumped at the sound of Holly's voice at the doorway to the veranda, waking Winston. The little dog nearly tumbled from his lap. As Isaac scrambled to catch Winston, he watched Holly stride across the veranda. He had to admit that she was extremely pretty, especially with the warm smile on her face. "Hi, Holly."

She collapsed into the chair Grace had used earlier and piled several shopping bags beside her. "So tell me all about it. Did the presentation go well? Did the kids enjoy it? Did you recruit a new generation of soldiers?"

"I wasn't trying to recruit anyone," Isaac answered.

Her easy grin and flippant tone vanished. "I'm sorry. I didn't mean to accuse you of anything. Are you all right?"

He ran a hand over his face. He shouldn't have snapped at her. "Sorry. The presentation went well. Thanks for asking."

"But you're not all right."

"I'm fine."

Holly frowned. "Liar. I thought we were getting to be friends. It's not nice to lie to your friends, especially at Christmas. You keep that up, buddy, and Santa will fill your stocking with coal."

"I'm an idiot," Isaac said.

"Well, that's a given, but don't feel bad about it. Most of the men I meet are." She smiled again and winked at him. "But really, what idiotic thing did you do?"

He avoided her gaze and stared across the lake. If he was going to admit to his idiocy, it couldn't be while he was looking into her eyes. "I guess I had formed an attachment to the person who wrote me so many kind letters," he said, his tone flat. "I don't think I even realized it, not completely. I was lying to myself. Anyway, I thought there was more behind the letters than there was."

Holly gasped, clearly realizing what he was trying to say. "You thought you'd found your soul mate."

He rolled his eyes. "I don't believe in soul mates, but I'm at a crossroads, I think."

"What do you mean?" she asked.

"When I went into the military, I assumed I'd stay until I retired," Isaac explained. "But lately I've begun to believe that's not the right call. At least not for me. I'm proud of the two tours I've done, but I'm also exhausted. I've seen too much. I've hurt too much. I want to come home, but if I leave the service, I'll be coming home to nothing and no one."

"And you hoped the woman who wrote you letters would change that," Holly said.

"So you see, I'm an idiot. She's married. And she wasn't feeling any of the things I imagined. She's simply a nice person who tried to make a soldier feel better. My grand plan was a ridiculous fantasy about a person who didn't really exist."

"That doesn't make you an idiot," Holly said. "It makes you a romantic."

"I'm not a romantic. Not after seeing the kinds of things I've seen." He shrugged. "Maybe it's for the best. It wouldn't be fair to drag another person into the chaos that my life will be. I don't know where I'm going. I don't even know what I want to do for a living."

"Wow," Holly said.

"I think my romantic fantasy was probably a way to make my decision easier," Isaac continued. "If I had someone to settle down with and start a family, then I'd know what the right decision was."

"So what do you see as your two options?" she asked.

"Stay in the service or leave," he replied, careful not to let his voice sound scornful of the question. He knew there was a lot of different choices before him, but they all boiled down to a simple binary, an on or off switch. Stay or go. Why couldn't he pick?

He hadn't realized that his annoyance was passing through his hands and into the pats he was giving Winston until the little dog glanced at him reproachfully and hopped down from his lap.

"Sorry, Winston," Isaac muttered.

Winston didn't return to Isaac's lap. Instead, he gazed hopefully at Holly.

"What are you good at?" Holly asked as she reached down to pet the dog. "What kinds of things do you enjoy? Computers? Writing? Working with your hands?" Then she let a touch of her teasing grin creep in. "Public speaking?"

"Definitely not public speaking." Isaac's hand brushed hers when he leaned forward to rub Winston's ear in apology. He jerked his hand back, surprised to find that the brief connection felt electric.

Clearly unperturbed by whatever undercurrents were going on with the humans around him, Winston trotted off the veranda to sniff at the grass beyond.

"Let's see." Isaac smiled slightly at Holly. "I excel at carrying heavy stuff. Probably from years of lugging heavy guns around."

"Okay, hotel bellman is in the mix," Holly said lightly. "But I think we should dig a little deeper. Is there anything else you did in the Army that you liked? Or anything from school?"

He considered her questions for a moment. "I did some electrical work in the Army. I'd been working with an electrician part-time when I enlisted, and the Army made use of that."

"So do you think you would enjoy being an electrician?" she asked.

"I did like it," Isaac agreed. "I actually thought about continuing even before I enlisted. The electrician hinted at a kind of mentoring program, but I was afraid I'd be stuck in Palmetto, Georgia, for the rest of my life. Don't get me wrong. There are a lot of good people there. But I wanted to see a bigger world, you know?"

"And have you?"

"Yes. I'm proud of the service I've done, and some of the things the Army let me see were amazing. I've been to museums in Europe, and I've touched a pyramid in Egypt." He tapped his temple. "It's not all bad memories in here."

"But you feel like you've met that need in your life?" Holly asked, her voice gentle. "That need to travel and explore?"

"For now at least." He huffed. "It's active duty that I'm done with. If I still wanted to serve, I could always go into the reserves. But the military life was my plan. It's all a little confusing."

She reached out and squeezed his hand. "If you want my opinion,

I think you already know what you need to do. Now you simply have to let yourself do it." Her teasing smile returned. "And there's a lot more to the Atlanta area than Palmetto. I love it there."

"You live in Atlanta?" Isaac asked.

Holly nodded. "We're practically neighbors." She gathered the pile of bags by her side. "Now, if you'll excuse me, I have to lug these upstairs and try to figure out which book to read first."

"More books?" Isaac teased. "You're not going to need help hauling your suitcase out of here, are you? Because if you're going to put even more books in it, I'm going to be busy that day."

Holly laughed. "I bought a tote bag just for the books."

"Because that solves the problem," he quipped.

"There's always a solution." Holly hopped up, clutching her bags. "Catch you at the social hour."

Isaac watched her stride off with a confidence he envied. He'd once had that confidence, and he would like to have it again.

As he gazed out at the lake, he realized that Holly had shown herself able to listen nearly as well as she could talk. Not only that, but he was starting to believe that he did have choices, a thought he hadn't had for a long time.

Isaac felt lighter. One thing he knew for sure was that he was in no hurry to leave the inn after all.

15

Ivy

When Holly had veered off to the veranda, Ivy nearly followed her, if for no other reason than to avoid Jolene's chatter. Ivy loved her friend, but her nerves felt frayed by Jolene's endless certainty that she was right about everything.

She caught a glimpse of one of the other guests outside—Isaac? Well, one of them should be happy, and Holly seemed to be developing a bit of a crush. With a last wistful glance at Holly's retreating back, Ivy climbed the elegant sweep of staircase with Jolene at her side.

"I'm glad you appreciate that dress I found for you," Jolene said.

"It is pretty," Ivy said. She had to admit that she loved the dress, and she would have never considered trying it on without pressure from her friend. "But I have no idea where I'll wear it."

"A dress like that can be versatile depending on your accessories," Jolene said. "It's the simple lines that do it."

As Jolene rattled on about fashion trends and classic styles, Ivy was surprised that she agreed with much of it.

Ivy had a fairly small wardrobe made up of carefully chosen pieces. She wanted to look good, but she also wanted to blend in and not draw too much attention, especially at social functions. Sometimes she worried that she wore the same dresses too many times to company functions. She shopped as rarely as she could manage, mostly from a feeling that it didn't matter very much. Ivy didn't have the elegant and unique style that Holly pulled off so effortlessly or the bold vivaciousness of Jolene. Ivy had always been a mouse among lions.

When they reached the second floor, Ivy glanced hopefully toward Jolene's suite door, but her friend was clearly planning to follow Ivy to her room.

With a sigh, Ivy gave in and opened her door. "I think I should rest for a few minutes. I feel the beginning of a headache coming on."

Jolene dropped into one of the comfortable chairs, letting her shopping bags drop beside her. "No problem. I'll only stay a minute. I wanted to make sure you're okay. You've been awfully quiet since we got here."

Ivy was surprised into a laugh. "You and Holly carry the conversation just fine without me."

Jolene leaned forward. "Are you calling us noisy?"

"More like enthusiastic," Ivy said. *Though noisy fits too.*

Jolene wrapped a strand of red hair around one finger. "It's been great getting together. I have friends in Charleston but no one like the two of you. We have real history, and we don't see one another nearly enough. I'm sorry it took something sad to bring us together. I hope you're feeling better."

Ivy wasn't sure that feeling better was even a possibility, but she nodded. "A little better. I'm glad we'll be spending Christmas together."

The last sentence was true at least. She was glad. If she couldn't have the romantic Christmas she'd envisioned with Ballard, then this was the best possible alternative. Holly and Jolene had been right about one thing—sitting alone in her apartment would have resulted in days spent in her pajamas watching bad TV and eating junk food.

Jolene got up and hugged Ivy, which was surprisingly comforting, until Jolene let her go and smirked at her. "I told you that getting together was the best thing for you. We'll help you get back on your feet and back on the plan."

Ivy barely stifled a groan. She was beginning to hate the plan, and she didn't want to talk about it anymore. "You and Holly are lifesavers. But now I'm going to take a nap. I haven't slept well in days."

Jolene peered at Ivy's face. "A nap would be good. I haven't figured out what we should do next, but I'm sure you don't want to do it with raccoon eyes. Besides, I think I'll go spend some quality time in the soaking tub in my room." She pointed at Ivy's bags. "But put those away first. You don't want wrinkles in your clothes."

"Yes ma'am," Ivy teased.

Jolene made a face at her as she grabbed her bags and sashayed toward the door.

Once Ivy closed the door on her friend, she nearly left her purchases in the bags out of pure stubbornness, but she didn't want her new clothes creased. She hung them carefully in the wardrobe before walking out onto the second-floor veranda and sinking down into one of the chairs there.

She admired the lake view. From this angle, the lake had become a serene pool of gold in the afternoon sun. As she watched, a pair of geese flew in noisily and landed on the lake, sending ripples across the liquid gold. *So much for serenity.*

Ivy rooted in the pocket of her jeans for a hair tie. She pulled her hair into a messy combination of ponytail and bun. It was far from stylish, but Ivy enjoyed the feel of the light breeze against the back of her neck.

As she watched the pair of geese, she wondered if they were like swans, mating for life. She loved the idea of finding one person to spend your life with. She had lost the belief that having someone serious in your life diminished you. *Surely I could be part of an us and still be me.* She'd truly thought that was possible with Ballard, but it had turned out to be a disaster.

Feeling restless, Ivy decided that she didn't want to lie down after all. Her racing thoughts would only keep her awake. No, what she needed was to walk until she was too tired to hear her brain chattering at her. Perhaps she would return to town and do some more window-shopping. She still had a couple hours before the inn's social hour. She'd probably enjoy the anonymity of being by herself in a town where she knew no one.

And maybe, just maybe, she'd find the guy who resembled Ballard and finally convince herself that she wasn't being haunted by a man who was most likely having a lovely Christmas with his new girlfriend in Charlotte.

As she stood and walked into her room, Ivy knew that her friends wouldn't let her go into town alone. At least one of them would offer to come along. From Jolene and Holly, offering could be a lot like insisting. It would be easiest on all of them if Ivy simply snuck out. She was surprised at how much the idea appealed to her.

Ivy grabbed her purse and slipped off her shoes so they wouldn't make a sound on the hardwood and give her away. Then she eased the door shut behind her and padded soundlessly to the stairs. She expected to run into Holly on the way down, but the stairs and foyer were empty. She put her shoes back on and made her escape.

Ivy knew she was being silly, but she found the feeling of adventure exhilarating, as if she'd shed years on the walk down the stairs and was now a naughty teenager. "I should sneak around more often," she murmured.

By the time she drove to downtown Magnolia Harbor and found a parking spot, the sun was going down. The old-fashioned streetlights had already switched on. The streetlights, combined with the Christmas lights in the store windows, gave the area a nearly magical glow.

In every window, Ivy admired the enticing displays. She felt content in the knowledge that she didn't need to buy anything. This was her favorite way to shop—with her eyes and without the pressure of needing something specific. In fact, she often window-shopped on her days off. After a few hours, she'd return to her apartment empty-handed but completely content simply to have enjoyed admiring pretty things.

With sunset, the temperature had dropped slightly, and eventually Ivy wished she'd brought a warm jacket, but she was enjoying herself too much to let the cold send her away. Instead, she ducked into the Dragonfly Coffee Shop to warm up and sip some hot chocolate. Once she was thoroughly warm, she'd return to the inn for social hour.

She perused the menu, now torn between a decadent hot chocolate or a mocha with nearly as much chocolate and cream. Finally, she decided on the mocha. She could use the boost of caffeine. She hadn't been lying to Jolene about the trouble she'd had sleeping lately.

Once she had her cup in hand, she turned to find a table and nearly ran right into a very ordinary man in a brown blazer. She knew that blazer nearly as well as she knew the gray eyes peering down at her.

Ballard Dorman.

Ivy stared at him, speechless. *I wasn't imagining things. Ballard really is here.*

For a moment, Ballard appeared shocked. But then he graced her with his extraordinary smile, so full of joy and warmth.

Ballard's smile reminded her of the sun coming out on a stormy day.

"Ivy," he murmured as if her name were something rare and wondrous. "I found you."

"Found me?" Ivy echoed. She suspected she sounded brainless, but she simply couldn't believe she was standing right in front of Ballard. She'd been so sure her glimpses of him had been brought on by her imagination. Unless this was some kind of psychotic break. Maybe she'd finally fallen over the edge and was now hallucinating.

"Ivy?" Ballard said, gently taking her arm. "You've gone pale."

She almost gasped in relief when she felt his warm hand on her arm. Ballard was real. She wasn't hallucinating.

"Come on. Let's sit down." He led her to a nearby table and helped her into a chair.

"You're actually here," she said softly, then felt completely idiotic about the words.

"I am."

"Why are you here?" she asked, recognizing how thin and high her voice sounded.

"I wanted to talk to you."

Ivy still couldn't understand what was happening. "But how did you know where to find me?"

Ballard's cheeks pinked slightly. "I went to your apartment, and you didn't answer the door. When I kept knocking, your neighbor came out and told me that you'd asked her to water your plants because you were going to Magnolia Harbor, South Carolina, for a reunion with college friends."

Ivy didn't know what to say, so she remained silent.

He shrugged slightly. "I didn't have any idea where you were staying, but I came anyway. I thought maybe I'd get lucky and find you if I searched hard enough. And now I have." Again, his smile lit his face.

"I'm staying at the Magnolia Harbor Inn with Holly and Jolene," Ivy said. She didn't know why she told him. It was simply something to say, and her mouth seemed to be running on automatic.

Ballard nodded. "I remember you telling me about them." He watched her closely. "Are they still rowdy?"

"They're exuberant," she protested, feeling defensive for her friends. "And loyal."

"Why do I feel there's a message for me in that comment?" he asked. "I've been calling and calling. Why did you stop taking my calls?

I thought we mattered more to each other than that. If you've met someone else and become serious with that person, I think I deserve to be told. You owe me an explanation."

"I sent you a text," Ivy whispered, suddenly feeling as if she didn't have enough breath to speak any louder.

"Not a particularly informative one," Ballard responded.

Without warning, tears filled her eyes. "I saw you with that woman at our table in our restaurant. I saw you."

The expression on Ballard's face turned confused, and he pressed his hands to the table as he leaned toward her. "I don't understand. I thought I was doing what you wanted."

"You thought I wanted another woman in my seat?" Ivy asked, finally speaking louder as his words stirred a surprising knot of anger in her chest.

"She was a client," he explained, then sighed. "Granted, I'm fairly sure she has more than a professional interest in me, but I honestly don't understand what's going on."

She blinked at him but didn't speak. She wasn't sure what was going on either. *A client?*

"You said that you wanted to keep our relationship casual," Ballard continued, annoyance mixing into his tone. "You said that I shouldn't imagine I had any claim on you."

Ivy almost whimpered. She recognized those words. They were the words she used whenever she dated anyone. The words Ivy, Jolene, and Holly had vowed to always say to keep their relationships free of drama so they could focus on their own lives. They were the words of the plan. And suddenly, Ivy hated them more than she'd ever hated anything in her life.

"You're right. It's true. It was all my fault." She hiccuped once as she fought to keep the tears at bay. "I ruined everything."

Ivy couldn't handle another second of Ballard's hurt, perplexed face, especially now that she knew she'd made her own misery. It was all her fault!

Despite knowing that she was completely to blame, she still didn't want to fall apart in public. She jumped out of her chair and ran for the door, narrowly avoiding a collision with a young man carrying two coffee cups.

Ballard called after her, but Ivy didn't even pause. She pushed her way through the door and kept running, threading through the shoppers and knowing they'd help cover her escape. She was being a huge coward, but she didn't care.

Finally, she made it to her car and jerked the door open, slamming it accidentally into her thigh with enough force to make her cry out.

Once Ivy was inside the car, she leaned on the steering wheel and gave into the storm of self-loathing and heartache and let the tears out.

She had driven Ballard away, and now it was too late to make amends. How could she have messed things up so much?

16

Grace

Though the evening was cool, the breeze was light enough for social hour to take place on the veranda again. Grace was glad. She wanted to spend as much time as possible outdoors before winter eventually forced them inside.

She was carrying a tray of stuffed mushrooms to the veranda as Holly and Jolene walked up from the shadowy lawn, wearing matching expressions of consternation.

"Have you seen Ivy?" Jolene asked.

Grace set the tray down on a table. "I haven't seen her since breakfast. Maybe she decided to do a little shopping."

"We've already been shopping," Jolene said. "If she wanted to go again, she could have asked us to go along."

"It is Christmas," Grace said gently. "It's a time for secret gift buying. Maybe that's why she didn't invite you. I can relate. I still need to do a little secret gift shopping of my own."

"I suppose that makes sense." Jolene took a plate from the table. She turned to Holly. "I didn't think we were doing a gift exchange."

"We didn't talk about it," Holly said as she accepted a glass of white wine from Grace. "But I admit that I wouldn't mind trading names and doing some Christmas shopping. Why wouldn't we want to exchange presents with our oldest friends?"

Jolene wrinkled her nose. "I'd rather you didn't use the word *oldest* in relation to me ever."

"I thought you were the realist," Holly teased.

"I'm not even thirty yet," Jolene retorted with a toss of her red hair. "I have a long time to go before I'm old."

"I should hope so," Grace chimed in. "Especially since I'm creeping uncomfortably close to fifty myself, and I don't see that as old."

"You're both right, of course. I was only joking." Holly popped a mushroom into her mouth.

Jolene groaned. "Still, that doesn't change the fact that I don't have anything for either of you. If we do exchange names, I'll have to go shopping tomorrow." She perked up. "Actually, it would be great to go shopping tomorrow."

Holly's laugh was merry. "That's the shopaholic we all know and love. So let's pick a person. How about I buy something for you? I think I totally get you."

"Fine, then I'll get something for Ivy," Jolene said. "She could use a little sprucing up. We'll tell her to get a gift for you."

"And then we'll all go shopping," Holly said with a grin.

"If you're downtown shopping tomorrow, you may want to be in the village green next to the lake by midafternoon," Grace suggested. "The high school band and carolers will be giving a concert. They're quite talented."

"That sounds good," Holly said. "We could go our separate ways for shopping in the morning, then meet there to hear the carolers. And if Ivy has been shopping and has it all out of her system, she can meet us for the caroling."

"I hope you'll be back here in the evening," Grace said. "You don't want to miss the social hour."

"I never miss a chance for wine," Jolene assured her.

The two women wandered over to the veranda chairs and sat, still chatting merrily.

Grace thought about how important long-term friendships could be. She had friends in Magnolia Harbor whom she'd known for many years. And, of course, her relationship with Charlotte was as both sisters and friends. *I'm so very blessed.*

Movement at her periphery drew Grace's attention to one of the French doors leading to the veranda, and she saw Isaac, clearly lost in thought.

When he wandered up to the table, Grace smiled at him. "What would you like to drink?"

"Just tea for me," he said. "I've never cared much for wine."

"I imagine it's an acquired taste," Grace said as she poured him a glass of tea from the tall glass pitcher. The golden tea in the pitcher seemed to glow in the lights of the veranda.

Isaac took the glass. "I don't think I'd enjoy the process of acquiring it." He took a long sip of tea. "But I could drink tea every day. Mine never comes out this perfect."

"We use high-quality tea," Grace said. "When you chill tea, it dulls our ability to taste it, so people use that as a reason to use cheaper tea. I personally think it still makes a difference."

Isaac took another long sip. "I think you're right."

Grace decided to risk a change of topic. "You look happier than when I saw you earlier. You must have recovered a bit from your grueling day."

"A bit," he said.

Grace was interested to note that his gaze drifted toward Holly.

"I'm sorry," Isaac said. "I shouldn't have even suggested walking out on my reservation here. I'll stay through my commitment, but I might not make it to the party."

"Oh, I do hope you will," Grace said. "I can promise the food will be delicious. Charlotte shines when it comes to holiday food."

He smiled. "I don't doubt it. My head is spinning with a lot of decisions right now, but none of them have anything to do with not appreciating this place. You have a wonderful inn, and I think you and your family are incredible."

"Thank you. I have to admit that I think so too." She was heartened to see her remark made Isaac's rather stiff smile soften into something much more comfortable on his open, friendly face.

"When I talked to the kids today, they were amazing," Isaac said. "I suspect your cousin deserves a lot of credit for that. Paisley's great. And I couldn't believe the efforts her dad went to. He drove to the school to give me a lift and jumped my car. You have a really caring family."

"Thank you," Grace said. "And remember, if you come to the party, you'll be an honorary part of that family."

"Sounds nice," he said.

Grace's heart sank at the wistful tone in Isaac's voice. He'd clearly gone back to whatever dark place he'd been in. Before she could figure out what to say, he lifted his glass to her and meandered away.

"Mom!"

Grace turned, her spirits lifting at the sound of Jake's voice.

Her son approached. "I was skimming the events on the flyer you gave me. I saw there's a British pantomime at the Jackson House Museum tonight. Do you want to go with me? We can catch some dinner afterward."

Grace smiled. "I would really enjoy that. Becky Thomas, the docent there, told me about the show. It sounds interesting."

Jake grinned. "Great. Now for some snacks." He began loading a plate enthusiastically. "I need to make sure I can last until a late dinner."

"As long as you leave some for the guests," Grace said, though she knew Charlotte always made more than enough food.

"Are you going to see the high school carolers tomorrow?" Jake asked. "I know how much you love caroling."

"I do, and I will absolutely make it if I can, but with the party the day after tomorrow . . ." Grace let her voice drift off. With the party so close, she should stay at the inn and work on preparations. She didn't even have gifts for the inn guests yet, so she'd have to shop the day before Christmas Eve, putting even more pressure on her.

"If I know you, you're worrying about something you already have well in hand," Jake said. "Honestly, what more do you have to do? Aunt Charlotte is doing the cooking, right?"

"She is, and I expect she'll appreciate an extra hand in the kitchen," Grace said, but she wasn't certain about that. Sometimes Charlotte seemed to prefer working alone when she was cooking. Plus, Grace suspected Dean would show up early, and he was sure to be a considerably better assistant than Grace. Of course, that was assuming Dean and Charlotte didn't end up squabbling over the menu.

Jake waved a hand in front of Grace. "Earth calling Mom. You checked out for a second there."

"I was thinking about tomorrow." Then she took a deep breath and smiled. "But I think I'll let tomorrow worry about itself."

"I'm surprised you and Aunt Charlotte aren't part of some adult caroling group," Jake remarked as he poured himself a glass of tea. "You both love to sing. In fact, you're the reason musicals never seemed all that weird when I was a kid. I had a mom who could burst into song at the drop of a hat."

"I do love to sing," Grace said. "But the church choir satisfies that for Charlotte and me. Not that I'm above singing while I clean. Still, I resent the implication that I made you feel like you lived in a musical."

Jake shook his head, then launched into a song. "Dust, dust, dust your room, gently with a rag. Get it clean before you play, and Mom won't be a nag."

Grace laughed. "I'd forgotten that one. In my defense, you were prone to letting dust build up in your room."

"Did I hear a dust song?" Isaac asked as he walked back to the table and refilled his tea glass.

"It was my mom's invention," Jake said, grinning. "You want to hear the second verse? It's about toilet bowl cleanliness."

"No!" Grace said, horrified. "If you sing that one, you aren't getting anything for Christmas."

"Too late. You said you already mailed my gift." Jake drew in a deep breath, opened his mouth, and started to belt out the next verse. "Swish, swish, swish—"

"That's enough singing." Grace grabbed one of Charlotte's garlic knots and pretended to shove it into Jake's mouth.

Jake and Isaac laughed together as they left the table and headed for chairs on the veranda.

Grace was glad to see the two young men talking and laughing, even if she was the butt of the joke. Maybe it would make Isaac feel better about the holiday party if Jake made friends with him.

"Did I hear Jake singing?" Charlotte asked as she walked out, carrying a fresh tray of stuffed mushrooms and garlic knots.

"You and everyone else," Grace said. "He has his father's ability to project."

"Has he told you what's bothering him?" Charlotte asked.

"I don't know that anything is bothering him," Grace replied. "He's an adult now and probably more serious because of that. Maybe you're sensing maturity, not problems."

Charlotte's eyes twinkled as she said, "Maturity demonstrated by the toilet bowl song."

"So you did hear it." Grace felt her cheeks warm. "It's enough to make me glad Spencer is out of town. At least most of the people who heard it live a long way from here."

"It's interesting that you thought of Spencer when you imagined people you wouldn't want Jake singing that song around," Charlotte said, her tone still playful. "And not, say, anyone from church or the chamber of commerce."

"Only because Spencer would probably tease me about it." Grace gave her sister a gentle poke. "Just like you."

"Right. Sure."

"You know Spencer and I are just friends," Grace said. "Keep it up, and I'll have a few things to say about you and Dean."

Charlotte raised both hands. "Okay, you win." She spun around and hurried back to the kitchen.

Grace idly straightened items on the table, making sure the napkins were neatly spread out and the glasses stood in precise rows. She glanced now and then at the guests, relieved to find that they all seemed happy. It gave her hope for the rest of the holiday week.

Ivy walked onto the veranda, glancing around hesitantly. She turned to Grace and offered her a weak smile.

The poor woman appears to have had a shock. Grace hoped she wasn't getting sick. There was nothing more miserable than being sick at the holidays, especially when far from home. "Would you like a glass of wine?" she asked as Ivy approached the table.

"White, please." Ivy's voice was quiet, almost a whisper, and the smile drifted from her face, leaving her even more ghostly.

Grace poured her a glass of wine, then handed it to her.

As Ivy accepted the wineglass, her hand trembled.

"Are you feeling all right?" Grace asked.

"I'm fine," Ivy answered. "But I have a bit of a headache."

"You should have something to eat," Grace urged. "That can help with a headache."

Ivy nodded and took a plate, adding hors d'oeuvres almost aimlessly. "I didn't eat much at lunch. That's probably the problem."

Grace was glad to note the young woman's voice sounded a little stronger, though she was still pale. Then Grace winced as Holly and Jolene spotted their friend, leaped out of their seats, and made a beeline toward Ivy.

"Ivy Lester," Jolene said, "you worried us half to death."

Ivy stiffened without turning around.

"I told them you'd probably been shopping," Grace whispered to Ivy. "Surprise shopping."

Ivy gave Grace a grateful smile, and then she faced her friends. "I was in town. It's almost Christmas, you know. Everyone has secrets."

"Well, I hope you didn't get both of us presents," Jolene said. "We've decided to draw names, and you get Holly. You'd better not turn up with a present for me too. I don't want to be the only one who follows gift exchange rules."

"We already know all about you," Holly said, giving her friend a sideways hug. "And seeing you is always gift enough."

"I know you're being sarcastic," Jolene said as she struck a pose. "But you have a point. Seeing me is terrific."

Holly studied Ivy. "You don't look so good."

"You still have a headache?" Jolene asked.

Ivy nodded. "Worse than ever, I'm afraid."

"I guess you should have taken that nap you mentioned instead of sneaking off," Jolene scolded.

"Come on, Ivy," Holly said. "Let's sit down. You can eat, and we'll tell you our ideas for what to do tonight."

Ivy frowned. "I don't suppose going to bed early is on the list."

"Poor darling, you must be exhausted," Holly said. "How about we have a quiet evening here?" She stopped and turned to Grace. "Did I read on the website that you have games and puzzles in the music room?"

"We do," Grace answered.

"Great," Holly said. "Remember the marathon backgammon games we used to have in college?"

Grace watched the trio huddle together to eat and talk. Though Ivy didn't seem to say much, she was clearly being agreeable. Grace was glad that Holly had shown some sensitivity to her friend. She suspected Ivy needed a good deal of that.

Maybe more than any of them knew.

Ivy

When Ivy woke the next morning, she realized she'd forgotten to draw the curtains the night before. In her apartment, she had heavy blinds to keep sunlight from waking her before the alarm went off. But this morning, light spread across the room like a promise, nudging Ivy out of her fretful dreams.

As she swung her legs over the side of the huge bed, she wondered if there was anything worth looking forward to about this Christmas. She had adored the holiday when she was a little girl and often spent the night before unable to sleep from pure excitement. She'd creep downstairs several times to peek at the piles of gifts under the twinkling tree. It was magical. Now it felt as if all the magic had drained out of this time of year and out of her life.

"Ballard," she whispered, "I miss you. I'm sorry I ruined everything."

A shower made her feel marginally more human, and careful makeup and clothing choices helped lessen her resemblance to walking despair.

Ivy regarded herself in the full-length mirror in her room. The cardigan she'd chosen was striped with shades of blue, from the palest ice-blue to periwinkle. She hoped the color would make her appear cheerier. She paired it with an A-line skirt that picked up one of the light blues of the cardigan. Underneath the cardigan, she wore a white blouse with a lace collar that made her skin tone seem slightly less pale. At least she had more color than the shirt.

She slipped into flats because she wasn't in the mood to deal with uncomfortable footwear. She still felt slow and heavy as she trudged down to breakfast. The formal dining room at the inn was brightly lit, mainly by the tall windows offering a view of the lake. The table was long enough to seat ten easily. Its polished dark wood was a stark contrast to the light hues in the rest of the room.

Holly was sitting at the table talking with Isaac and Jake.

As Ivy took a seat next to her friend, she was careful not to let her relief show. "Is Jolene okay?"

"As far as I know," Holly said. "I knocked on her door, and something growled at me to go away until a respectable hour. I'm fairly sure it was either Jolene or a bear."

Grace and Charlotte entered the room with plates of French toast.

"Good morning," Grace said, setting plates in front of Ivy and Holly. "Sorry to keep you waiting."

"No problem," Holly answered. "We just got here."

Charlotte handed Jake and Isaac their plates, then gestured to the sideboard. "There's orange juice and coffee over there. Can I get anyone a cup of coffee?"

"Yes please," Holly and Ivy said together, then grinned at each other.

As Charlotte poured their coffee, she asked, "Where's Jolene?"

"She's sleeping in," Holly said.

Charlotte smiled as she gave them their cups. "Her breakfast will be waiting for her in the kitchen."

"Please let us know if you need anything," Grace said, then left the room with her sister following.

Holly took a bite of her French toast. "This is really good."

Ivy glanced down at her breakfast. "I'm sure it is, but I'm not hungry." She cast her gaze toward one of the long windows at the end of the room. "Jolene's missing a lovely morning."

"You say that with all the enthusiasm of a guilty woman on the way to the gallows," Holly said. "I'm so sorry for your broken heart. You do know that, right?"

Ivy smiled. "It was my own fault. I brought it all on myself." Tears welled in her eyes, and she dashed them away, not caring about her makeup. But she was glad that Jake and Isaac were deep in conversation and didn't seem to be paying attention to what she was saying to Holly.

"Please talk to me," Holly said. "I want to help."

"I ruined everything," Ivy mumbled.

Holly frowned. "I thought it was Ballard who decided he wanted to date another woman at the same time as you."

"Because I suggested it." Ivy's voice was choked, and the words almost refused to come out.

"What?"

"Well, not in so many words. I parroted the ridiculous lines that Jolene is so fond of, the nonsense about keeping our relationship light and unrestricted, about freedom." Ivy sighed. "I know all of that works for Jolene, but it resulted in misery for me. I finally found someone I could have spent the rest of my life with."

"Really?" Holly asked.

Ivy waved a hand. "Maybe. I don't know, but I know I ruined it. He went out with another woman because I basically told him to do it."

"How do you know all this?" Holly asked. "Is it something you just now worked out? Because you could be wrong."

Ivy shook her head. "Ballard is in Magnolia Harbor."

"Are you kidding?"

"No. I spotted him at The Tidewater before the comedy show, and I saw him downtown when we were shopping. I thought I was hallucinating, but then I bumped into him at a coffee shop when I went to window-shop on my own. That was when we talked and I found out what a total fool I've been."

"Why is he here?" Holly asked.

"He said he wanted to talk to me. He asked my neighbor where I was, and he came searching for me. I hadn't been exactly clear in my breakup text to him. He wanted closure."

Holly's eyes grew round. "He came to Magnolia Harbor, missing his own Christmas, to hunt for you? I'm sure there's more to it than just closure."

"Like I said, the text I sent confused him. And Ballard is a tidy man. He probably wanted an answer that would make sense to him. Not that I managed to give him an answer yesterday. I flipped out and ran away from him."

"Wait a minute," Holly said. "I'm not sure you're reading this right. He went to a lot of effort simply to get an answer. Especially an answer that he could have gotten through a phone call or a text."

"I haven't been answering his calls," Ivy admitted.

"I think you need to talk to him—*really* talk to him," Holly said. "He needs to be asked point-blank why he came to find you and what he wants."

"It's too late," Ivy said. "Ballard told me that the woman he'd gone out with was a client, but she wants more than a working relationship with him. I could tell that by the way she leaned toward him and touched his hand that night. Ballard went out with her because of the silly things I'd said. He told me so."

"He dated someone he didn't want to date?" Holly wrinkled her nose. "And you want to get back with this guy?"

"I think I love him."

"I strongly suggest you don't say that to Jolene," Holly responded. "You know how she is about the plan, and love doesn't factor into it."

Ivy gaped at Holly for a moment, not sure what to say. Finally, she stammered, "Y-you say that as if you're not completely in agreement with Jolene."

"When have I ever been completely in agreement with Jolene?" Holly laughed. "My dear Ivy, we're not college girls anymore. Life is much more complicated than we thought back then. At least, I know my life has been." She smiled a little. "I'm not sure about Jolene's life. I'm not sure it would dare to be complicated."

Ivy almost smiled. "That's true."

"I think you need to keep all your options open so that you can have the life that's right for you," Holly went on. "We don't have to be Jolene, and I doubt we could be even if we tried. And that's perfectly okay."

"I never knew you felt that way," Ivy said. "I always assumed you were totally in step with her."

"Jolene marches to the beat of her own rather odd drummer, and that's fine," Holly said. "It clearly works for her. But you don't have to have the same life as Jolene or anyone else for that matter. You need to do what's right for you. And I'll always be on your side when it comes to you being happy."

Ivy reached for Holly's hand and gave it a squeeze. "Thank you. That means a lot to me."

"Don't forget that Jolene will be on your side too."

"You think so?" Ivy couldn't hide the incredulity in her voice.

Holly laughed again. "She'll rant for a while at first, but eventually she'll be on your side. Jolene loves you. So do I. It just takes Jolene a little longer to get used to the idea that she's not in charge of everyone."

Ivy had to chuckle at how astutely Holly knew Jolene but also how well she handled the steamroller that Jolene could be. Ivy wasn't sure if she could do that, but maybe she needed to try. Or try for the future, since Ivy was absolutely certain there was nothing to do about the present beyond being miserable. "I wish you had explained all this to me years ago."

"Wishes don't make miracles," Holly said. "But sometimes action does. Right now we need to figure out what you can do to fix this and patch things up with Ballard. It's time we made a plan of our own."

"I appreciate it, but it's not going to work. I've ruined everything with Ballard."

"I seriously doubt that," Holly said. "A man doesn't go to as much trouble as he has when there's no hope."

"You don't know Ballard," Ivy protested. "He's a guy who needs to understand things. He likes order. He wants answers and closure."

"And I think you're underestimating him," Holly said. "The exact same way you underestimated me and Jolene. He tracked you down. He cares."

"But that doesn't matter," Ivy said. "I don't even know where he's staying."

"Call him and find out."

"I deleted everything about him from my phone," Ivy replied. "His contact information, photos, everything. I thought clearing it all away would give me a fresh start. Instead, it felt as if I'd killed something."

"When was this?" Holly asked.

"The day we got here." Ivy reached into her jacket pocket and held up her phone. "And see? He hasn't called since I saw him yesterday. If what you said about him was true, why would he stop calling?"

"I say we ask him that question." Holly dabbed at her mouth with her napkin, then jumped up and grabbed Ivy's hand. "We need to find him."

"Now?" Ivy yelped.

"I don't know of a better time," Holly said. She turned to Jake and Isaac, who were still talking to each other. "Please excuse us." Then she proceeded to drag Ivy into the kitchen.

The room was bright and spacious and easily the most modern room that Ivy had seen in the inn, with gleaming stainless steel appliances and impressive-looking gadgets that Ivy couldn't have identified. Nearly every counter was covered with bowls or pots or piles of fresh vegetables.

Grace and Charlotte stood at separate counters doing some mysterious cooking things. At least their actions were mysterious to someone like Ivy whose main kitchen appliance was a microwave.

When Ivy and Holly burst into the kitchen, Charlotte spun around and stared at them with alarm on her face. "Is something wrong with the breakfast?"

"No, the French toast was amazing," Holly said. "I don't know how you manage to create something that tastes so light yet so decadent. But that's not why we're here. We want to know about other places to stay in Magnolia Harbor."

Now it was Grace's turn to look alarmed. "Do you want to move to a different inn?"

Ivy shushed her friend before she could give Grace and Charlotte something else to panic about. "No, we want to find a man who is staying somewhere in Magnolia Harbor. And we need to know the scope of the places he might be."

Grace pressed her hand to her heart. "Thank goodness. You had me worried. I don't want to chase away any of our guests, especially so close to Christmas. Would this man choose inexpensive lodging?"

Ivy shook her head. "Ballard makes good money, and he's not tight with it. He'd want to stay somewhere nice."

"Maybe he's staying at The Tidewater," Charlotte said.

"I did see him there on the night of the comedy event," Ivy said. "But I don't think he was able to get into the show."

Charlotte frowned. "In that case, I take my suggestion back. He can't be staying there. Dean wouldn't have allowed one of his guests to be turned away."

"There aren't many other nice places," Grace said. "A few bed-and-breakfasts. Would he have wanted to stay inside Magnolia Harbor?"

"If he could," Ivy said.

Grace wiped her hands on a towel and picked up a notepad and a pen from the kitchen island. "Let me write a list of the smaller inns and their addresses. I assume you're planning to visit them in person. I could give you their phone numbers, but no one will talk about guests over the phone."

"We're intending to go to them," Holly said. She took the list as soon as Grace finished it. "If you see Jolene while we're gone, please don't mention the inns, okay?"

Grace winced. "I hate to lie to a guest."

Holly smiled. "Tell her we've gone searching for Ivy's heart's desire. That's true enough."

"In that case, mum's the word," Grace said. "And I hope you find it."

Ivy's eyes filled again unexpectedly. "I hope so too."

18

Grace

After removing the last of the freshly cleaned breakfast plates from the dishwasher and drying them, Grace carried the stack over to the cupboard. "Are you sure you're all right with me running into town?"

"I'll be fine," Charlotte assured her as she stretched plastic wrap over the bowl of stuffing. "I have a precise schedule for today's prep. It's actually easier if I can work my plan without further interruption."

Grace didn't take offense at Charlotte's suggestion that Grace was a potential hindrance. She knew how stressed her sister became when preparing for big events. At least the Christmas party tomorrow was mostly family and inn guests, people who were more forgiving of mistakes. She said as much.

Charlotte gaped at her. "You've got to be kidding. No one is more judgmental than family when it comes to traditional events like holiday dinners."

"No one is going to judge you," Grace insisted.

"Maybe not to my face," Charlotte grumbled, then walked to the fridge and began collecting vegetables from the crisper. "But someone will."

"I'm sure everyone is going to love what you make," Grace said.

Charlotte didn't seem convinced. She retrieved a cutting board from the cabinet, then asked, "Oh, how was the pantomime last night?"

"It was very entertaining," Grace said. "Jake and I had a great evening together."

"I'm glad you had the chance to spend some time with him before everything gets even crazier."

"Me too," Grace said. "I'll be back to help you as soon as I buy presents for the guests. Family has been sneaking in and piling gifts under the tree. It's going to take forever to open all of them, and I don't want the guests feeling left out."

"You have a soft heart," Charlotte told her. "And you're brave. I wouldn't want to go shopping the day before Christmas Eve."

"It'll probably be quiet," Grace said. "Everyone will have finished their shopping long ago."

Charlotte laughed. "Clearly you don't usually shop this close to Christmas. Have a good time. And don't let anyone take stuff away from you."

"Take stuff away from me?" Grace stared at her sister. "What kind of town do you think Magnolia Harbor is?"

Still chuckling, Charlotte said, "A normal one." Then she flipped over a recipe card in front of her and yelped. "Oh no!"

"What's wrong?" The question was said in unison by Grace and Jake who'd come through the kitchen door.

Charlotte gave them a panicked look. "I don't have enough oranges for the orange and cranberry sauce, and I have to get it done today so it can have time for the flavors to meld together in the fridge. Would one of you go get some?"

"I can," Grace said. "But it will be a while before I get back since I really need to pick up those presents."

"More presents for me?" Jake teased. "I don't want anything to get in the way of that. I'll go get the oranges, even if I have to search high and low."

"The searching won't take that long," Charlotte answered. "Hanson's Farm Fresh Foods is holding a box of oranges for me. I forgot to pick it up. But you'll need to get it soon so I can get the sauce on."

"Yes ma'am." Jake reached out to snag a strip of bacon.

Charlotte swatted at his hand. "That's not for you. I'm using it in the bacon and cheddar mini quiches for this evening's social hour."

"Hey, I need sustenance for going out in the cold," Jake protested.

"It's a trip to the grocery store, not a hike through the snow," Charlotte said. "Now go."

"Tyrant," Jake grumbled as he headed for the door.

Grace watched her son leave the kitchen. She was beginning to sense what Charlotte had been talking about. Jake was the same friendly guy he always was, but something about it didn't seem as light and easy as usual. It was almost as if Jake were working at being his normal self.

Or maybe she'd listened to Charlotte for too long, and now she was imagining things.

"I'll be back soon," Grace said, grabbing her keys and her purse.

Winston bounded into the room and danced around her feet, obviously hoping to go along.

"Sorry." Grace bent to pet the dog. "But you have to stay here."

Winston flopped on the floor and sighed, making the sisters laugh.

Grace left, still a bit bemused. Charlotte certainly was being fanciful lately, first suspecting that something was wrong with Jake and then thinking Magnolia Harbor would be stressed and grumpy at Christmas. That was ridiculous.

Like Charlotte, Grace had done her time in the much larger city of Charleston, which had its own special charm and many more people. Grace had worked for Maddox Creative, one of the country's largest marketing firms, and Charlotte had been a sous-chef and then head chef at Le Crabe Fou. They both knew the chaos of holiday time in a big city, but Magnolia Harbor wouldn't be that way at all. Grace knew that Charlotte was wrong, and it would be a nice, quiet morning.

It didn't take Grace long to realize that Charlotte was right. The sidewalks were crowded with people, and unlike bustling days throughout the holiday season, the shoppers had a desperate edge. *I don't suppose anyone puts off shopping to the last minute on purpose.* Grace kept that in mind whenever someone cut in line ahead of her or jostled her on the sidewalk.

Finally, Grace took a break on a bench near The Book Cottage. She'd bought two lovely pewter bookmarks with matching book lights for Holly and Ivy and a delicate glass dip pen from the art section of the bookstore for Jolene. She wasn't sure a graphic artist ever did traditional art these days. Computers seemed to be the order of the day for that sort of thing, but she had been taken by the elegant beauty of the pen. Maybe Jolene would appreciate it for the decor possibility if nothing else.

Now if only she could find something for Isaac. Grace gazed gloomily at the passersby. She was already tired of being bumped into, and she had no idea where to find a gift for the young soldier. "I should have asked him more questions about what he enjoyed," she muttered under her breath. "Or downloaded Jake's Gift Assistant."

"Grace!"

She turned toward the shout and spotted Dean Bradley weaving through the crowd with an expression of clear relief.

He collapsed onto the bench beside her as soon as he'd breached the crowd. "I'm so glad to see you."

"Why is that?" Grace asked.

"I want to give something to Charlotte, but I'm completely stumped," Dean said. "It's not like I've never bought a present for a woman, but I can't use my two go-to gifts."

"And they are?" Grace asked.

"I usually buy flowers or jewelry," he said. "But neither of those works for Charlotte. You guys always have plenty of flowers at the inn, so you don't need mine. And Charlotte doesn't wear much jewelry."

"She has a few pieces that matter a lot to her," Grace said. "Mostly from our mother. But she has her hands in food too much for rings and bracelets."

"So you see my problem. I want to give her something. It's nice that she invited me to your Christmas party, and I like Charlotte. We have our rivalries, but I admire her as a chef and a friend."

"I would think that no one would be able to pick a gift for Charlotte better than another chef," Grace said. "You both have cooking in common."

"Yeah, and I know how perfectly outfitted your kitchen is," Dean said. "So what do you buy a chef who already has everything?" He slumped slightly. "I don't want to go empty-handed, but if I buy something boring or useless to her, I'm going to feel like a goof."

"In that case, you may want to consider something symbolic," Grace suggested.

He sat up straighter. "Symbolic?"

"Yes. You and Charlotte have known each other for years now. How do you see your friendship? If you had to sum it up in a word or two, what would it be? Then think of an object that symbolizes that."

Dean's eyes lit up, and he laughed. "Of course. I think I've got just the thing." He jumped up and grabbed Grace's hands, nearly knocking her package from her lap. "Thanks so much. You've saved the day. I'll see you later." Dean spun and disappeared into the milling crowd.

Grace stared after Dean, wishing she'd asked him for a gift suggestion for Isaac. Then she thought of Jake. He'd been talking with Isaac. Maybe he'd have some good ideas.

Grace stood and smoothed a wrinkle from her pants. She'd go back to the inn and enlist Jake in the search for a nice gift for Isaac, and everything would be fine.

With that load off her mind, she gripped her shopping bag and braved the crush to go home.

19

Jake

After dropping the oranges off in the kitchen and running upstairs before Charlotte could rope him into any more chores, Jake gave into the temptation to open his laptop. He soon regretted it.

In fact, Jake closed his laptop after pointedly ignoring another round of e-mails. If he kept this up, the problem of what to do might resolve itself. That wasn't what he wanted, but at least it would take the pressure off him.

For a moment, Jake had an old memory of his dad telling him that a man tackled his problems, even if he had to find a creative solution. Jake couldn't remember what he'd done to get that talk, but he assumed his dad would say the same thing right now if he were around.

"I wish you were, Dad," he said softly. "I could sure use a creative solution right now."

His memories of his dad were all blurry snippets, and some memories he suspected came from stories he'd been told rather than true recollections of his own. He knew that was normal. Jake had been a toddler when his dad died in a train accident. But his mom had been great, and he always felt surrounded by love and support from his family. *Still, I wouldn't mind a little advice from Dad right now.*

Despite his faith in his mom's wisdom, Jake wasn't ready to talk about his problem with her. He knew she would have a hard time being impartial about the decision he had to make, and she'd tie herself in knots trying to be. But his mom wasn't the only source of wisdom in Jake's life or in his family.

His great-aunt had always been a source of good advice for both his mom and his aunt. Mom often told Jake about things Aunt Winnie said or ways she helped guests at the inn. Jake figured if his great-aunt was that helpful to his mom, maybe she could give him some advice as well.

He grabbed his jacket from the chair he'd tossed it over and headed out the door. This time he'd pass on using the back stairs because he was almost certain to run into either his mother or his aunt in the kitchen. He slowed down when he reached the winding stairs from the second floor to the first and crept down slowly to ensure his footsteps were quiet. It wasn't that he was hiding from his mother and aunt, but he preferred to get out of the house without a long conversation. He'd avoided that over breakfast, and he wanted to keep the streak running.

When he reached the bottom of the steps, he discovered Winston waiting for him, his expression eager.

"Sorry, pal," Jake said. "I can't take you with me. But I promise to throw a ball for you when I get back."

He knew the little dog couldn't have understood his words, but Winston must have recognized the tone because he immediately drooped before trudging off toward the kitchen.

Wow, Winston is even better at making me feel guilty than Mom.

Once outside, Jake zipped up his windbreaker against the chilly air and turned toward his great-aunt's house. He could have driven, but it wasn't a long walk. He headed down the long drive from the house to Lake Haven Road, taking deep breaths of the fresh morning air as he walked.

He didn't take morning walks in Raleigh. As he'd told his mom, he actually used to go running on the trails around the company where he worked, but he'd fallen out of the habit now that his workload was so heavy. He needed to start running again. There was something about morning air that seemed to help clear his head.

When Jake caught sight of his great-aunt's house across the road, he crossed quickly and trotted up the steps to the small front porch. He tapped on the front door, unsure of the proper etiquette for relatives who didn't come home all that often.

The door opened, and a young teenager peered at him through overgrown bangs. She wore a bulky gray sweatshirt with an alien stenciled on the front and flannel pants. She shuffled her feet, clad in bunny slippers, as she squinted at him. "Do I know you?"

"Hi, Sarah," Jake said, recognizing his cousin immediately. Sarah was the daughter of Adam Holland and Winnie's daughter Maria. They lived in Nashville, and Jake didn't see them much. "You've gotten taller. I'm your cousin Jake. Grace is my mom."

"Hi." Sarah offered him a lopsided smile.

"Is your grandmother around?" Jake asked.

Sarah nodded and backed up to let him in. "In the dining room making stuff with Sam and Monica. I'm probably going to help too, but I just got up, and I haven't had breakfast."

"Sleeping in is what vacations are all about," Jake said.

"I know, right?" she said, brightening considerably.

Sarah led him into the dining room, where the smell of cinnamon tickled the inside of Jake's nose, threatening to make him sneeze. At the table, Monica Russell stood on a chair in order to reach a collection of cookie cutters. Her brother, Sam, stirred a bowl of some kind of lumpy batter while their mom, Paisley, poured cinnamon into the bowl.

"Jake!" Paisley exclaimed. She set the can of cinnamon down and ran around the table to throw her arms around Jake, engulfing him in the scent of cinnamon and apple. Then she stepped back. "I heard you were home. I figured I wouldn't see you until tomorrow night at the party. What are you doing here?"

Jake smiled. Though Paisley was close to his mom's age, he'd always felt they had a lot in common. Paisley was comfortable around computers and software and had never viewed Jake's job as something mysterious and slightly odd the way some of the family did.

"I hoped to chat with Aunt Winnie." He nodded toward the spread on the table. "Are you guys making cookies?"

The question was answered by giggles from Sam and Monica.

"These cookies would taste yucky," Monica said.

"They do," Sam agreed. "I tasted them."

"I told you the dough is for ornaments, not eating," Paisley chided her son.

Sam shrugged. "I know, but I like applesauce." Then he wrinkled his nose. "But it's not good with all the spicy stuff."

"Don't feel bad," Sarah told him. "I tasted the cinnamon dough when I was a kid too. It smells a lot better than it tastes."

"We're making ornaments for the Christmas tree at the inn," Monica explained. "Mom says it'll make it smell good."

"And she's right," Winnie said as she walked into the room. Though a petite woman, barely five foot three, Winnie had a presence about her, the air of someone with wisdom and grace. Jake noticed that her thick blonde hair had a few more gray streaks than he remembered, but her eyes had the same kindness. "The smell of cinnamon will help even the loneliest guest feel at home. So, Jake, are you going to come here and hug me?"

Jake rounded the table, dodging cousins and chairs. He put his arms around his tiny aunt, careful not to hug her too tight. Her own hug was heartier.

When she released him, Jake responded to her earlier remark. "What makes you think any of the guests are lonely? I met them all, and they seem happy enough. And the three women came together, so they're not here alone."

"Holidays can be hard on people," Winnie said, then tilted her head to one side, giving Jake the impression of a curious bird. "Sometimes a person feels the loneliest of all when he's in a group of loved ones while harboring a secret."

Jake felt his cheeks burn. He should have known that Aunt Winnie would be able to see right through him. He'd come to talk to her because of her keen discernment, but he hadn't taken into account how uncomfortable that same trait could be. "You seem busy around here. Do you have time to chat with your favorite great-nephew?"

"I can make time," Winnie said. "Come and have a cup of coffee with me." She led him into the kitchen, which was blissfully empty.

Jake caught a hint of chocolate in the air. He was surprised that he could smell anything else after the barrage of cinnamon. "It smells good in here."

"It's my chocolate torte," Winnie said as she walked over to the coffee maker. She poured two mugs of coffee. "I finished it right before you came. I'll be bringing it to the party tomorrow, if I can keep it safe around here until then."

"Sounds delicious," Jake said, taking a seat at the table. "I'll make sure I save space for it."

Winnie carried the mugs over to the table and sat down across from Jake. "You wanted to talk to me about something? Something you didn't want to say in front of everyone?"

"Well, yeah, but only because I haven't told Mom yet. If she thought everyone knew before her, she'd be hurt. But she'd understand about my talking to you. Everyone talks to you."

Winnie smiled at him over the rim of her mug, her eyes twinkling. "Flatterer."

Jake hadn't meant it to be flattery, just honesty, but he decided not to comment. Instead, he got right to the point. "I've been offered a job."

"Don't you have a job?"

"I do. And I love it." Jake paused, suddenly unsure of how to approach the situation. "Did you know I was the lead programmer for the Gift Assistant app?"

His great-aunt nodded. "Your mother told me. She is proud of you, even if she doesn't understand your job well."

"Yeah, I know. Gift Assistant has been a runaway best seller. It's performed better than they ever expected, and sales haven't slowed down at all, which is unheard of. It's a pretty big deal."

"That's wonderful. Congratulations."

"Thanks," he said. "Anyway, now another company has come to me with a job opportunity. They're offering a huge pay increase and a big jump in responsibility."

"Sounds impressive," Winnie said. "What would you be doing in this new position?"

"Less hands-on programming and more team leading," Jake said. "But it would be a giant leap in my career, something I couldn't have expected for another decade probably."

Winnie clapped. "Good for you. You deserve it." Then she held her hands together and leaned closer to him. "But it's not all good news, is it?"

"The company is in China. The job would be there too." He took a sip of coffee as he waited for her reaction.

"Oh my."

"It's not that I don't want to see the world. I love the idea of travel. And this company is highly regarded." Jake set his mug down and stared into it, the blackness of the coffee reminding him of the swirl of emotions he felt.

Winnie set her own mug down and touched Jake's hand. "You sound as if you're trying to talk yourself into something. You've told me the pluses. So what are the minuses?"

"I'll be a long way from home, of course."

Winnie waved that off. "Planes fly everywhere, and I can tell by your voice that isn't your main minus."

He shook his head. "I feel that it should be one of the main ones. I love my family, and Mom would be torn up."

"Your mother would be proud of your success," Winnie said firmly. "And she misses you like crazy now with you in Raleigh. Away is away."

"I guess," Jake said. "But I'm happy in my job right now. I enjoy the hands-on stuff and the complexity and challenge of coding. And I like living in Raleigh. It's a beautiful city."

"And you're not sure the new job will offer those things?"

"I don't know. I don't want to give up what I have only to discover I'm a long way from home in a country where I don't speak the language, and I'm lonely."

"I believe a lot of Chinese people speak English," his aunt said mildly. "It's taught to children in school." She leaned across the table to squeeze his hand again. "What do you want me to do?"

Jake groaned. "I don't know. Tell me what to do."

Winnie's face brightened. "Follow your heart, and tell your mother."

"It sounds easy."

"It's simple, not easy," Winnie countered. "Now sit right there. I have something you can do for me." She hurried out of the room before he could respond.

Jake sat back in his chair and returned to sipping his coffee. The bitter taste usually felt as if it were sharpening Jake's senses, but today it seemed like one more unpleasant thing he was subjecting himself to, so he set the coffee on the table again.

When his great-aunt returned, she was carrying a wrapped package. "I need you to give this to your mother. It's for the soldier who is staying at the inn. I picked it up at a yard sale. It's used, but it isn't too banged up. And I think he needs it."

"Couldn't you bring it when you come tomorrow night?" Jake asked.

"I'll have my hands full with the torte." Winnie's smile turned mischievous. "Unless you think I should leave the torte behind in favor of this."

"I wouldn't like that at all," he said. "But I also know you're going to be leading a whole parade over to the house with Paisley and Maria and their families. I'm guessing at least one of them will have free hands."

"Are you trying to be difficult, young man?" Aunt Winnie asked with mock severity. "You don't have to ask questions about everything. As I remember, you were endlessly curious as a little boy."

"Asking questions about everything is what got me where I am today," he said.

"Worried and confused?" she teased.

Jake laughed. "Not that part, but I was fascinated by computer programs all my life. I wanted to know how they worked. And that's led me to where I am. And I'm good at what I do."

"I don't doubt that for a moment." Winnie gave him a kiss on the cheek. "Now take this to the inn and give it to your mother. And while you're at it, tell her what you're wrestling with."

"Okay, okay." He took the package from Winnie but nearly dropped it, as the weight was a surprise. "What did you get him? Cast iron?"

She smiled. "You'll see tomorrow night when we all unwrap presents."

"Well, Isaac is going to win the prize for the heaviest Christmas gift," Jake joked.

Still smiling, his aunt shooed him from the kitchen.

As Jake passed through the dining room, he stopped to admire several of the cinnamon ornaments. The kids had been painting them with thick white and pink paint, giving them the appearance of icing. "They look great."

"I'm only doing trains," Sam said. "No girlie shapes."

"Stars aren't girlie," Sarah said. "Don't be a chauvinist."

"What's that?" Sam asked suspiciously.

Jake leaned over and whispered, "Guys who say *girlie* as if it's an insult. Right now, it's only going to annoy your family. But trust me, it's not going to help your dating life when you get older."

"Dating life?" Sam repeated. "Eww."

Jake laughed. "Yeah, check back with me in ten years and let me know if you still feel that way." He carried the package outside and spotted his cousin Maria coming up the walk with a bag from the convenience store nearby.

"Jake! How nice to see you." She gave him a hug with her free arm, then hefted the bag. "I had to run out for coffee creamer. We have a lot of folks drinking coffee here. What brought you over?"

"I wanted to talk to your mom," he said. "I have a tough decision to make, and I don't seem to be getting any closer to making it. I was hoping Aunt Winnie would give me the answer."

Maria laughed. "And how did that work out for you?"

"I still have a tough decision to make," Jake admitted.

"Yeah, Mom isn't into easy answers." She paused. "You want to know what I do when I have a difficult decision and can't seem to find the answer that will work for me?"

"Sure," he said, hoping her answer would be more specific than following his heart.

"I flip a coin."

"Really?" Jake asked skeptically.

Maria held up her hand and added, "I flip a coin, and when it makes the decision for me, I check how I feel about the choice the coin made. If I'm relieved, it was the choice I wanted most. Sometimes the one I was keeping secret even from myself. And if I'm disappointed, I know I should make the other choice instead."

"And that works for you?"

"When I was trying to decide if I ought to change my life completely, I flipped a coin," she answered. "And today I'm happily married with the two best teenagers in the world."

"Thanks," Jake said. "I'm not sure I'm ready to make this decision with a coin yet, but you've given me something to think about."

In truth, he thought Maria's idea was kind of silly, but as he trudged back to the inn, he had to admit that it was as good of an idea as any he'd had so far.

He'd barely gotten to the street when a familiar voice called his name.

Jake turned to see Paisley jogging down the sidewalk with a large tin box in her hands. He recognized the box. Aunt Winnie filled it with homemade candy every year.

"Mom told me to carry the fudge over so we'd have one less thing to bring tomorrow," Paisley explained. "But I think it's mostly to get the temptation away from her. She loves fudge."

Jake didn't mind the company for the walk back to the inn, especially since Paisley had never been the sort to pry. Instead, she filled the silence with tales from school. He found the chatter surprisingly soothing. It distracted him from his decision, and that was fine with him.

20

Charlotte

Charlotte stared at the growing pile of dishes in the sink, knowing she should stop and take care of them before the kitchen got completely out of hand.

She wondered when Grace and Jake would return. Charlotte didn't want anyone trying to interfere with her cooking, but she was all for putting family to work on cleanup and prep. She had already gone to Jake's room to see if he'd lend a hand, only to discover her nephew had slipped out unnoticed.

Though the party was still more than twenty-four hours away, Charlotte's to-do list was far too long. She wasn't whittling it down nearly fast enough.

The kitchen door swung open, and Charlotte felt a rush of relief as she turned, expecting to see either Grace or Jake. She wasn't picky about which one.

Instead, Jolene strode into the kitchen, with a young Chinese woman following her.

"This woman was in the foyer. She's hunting for Jake." Jolene stepped back to stand in the doorway, clearly not intending to miss out on whatever happened next.

"Are you a friend of Jake's?" Charlotte asked, wondering briefly if the pretty young woman could be Jake's girlfriend. Could this woman be the reason Jake had been acting a bit off?

"No," the stranger said, shattering Charlotte's musing. "I am Michelle Wong. And you are?"

Charlotte eyed the young woman for a moment before answering, put off by the tone of the question. She guessed Michelle to be in her early twenties, like Jake. She wore her glossy black hair in a long ponytail, which Charlotte would have called a casual style on anyone else, but somehow Michelle managed to pull it off without a hair out of place. She wore a smartly tailored business suit in dove gray, and her makeup was flawless. Despite being several inches shorter than Charlotte, the woman managed to carry an intimidating air.

"I'm Charlotte Wylde, Jake's aunt. I can't tell you where he is at the moment. He didn't leave an itinerary. May I ask why you want to talk to him?"

"I should speak to him first." Michelle opened a small purse and retrieved a business card. "Perhaps you could give him this. I very much need to talk to him today."

Charlotte took the card. It wasn't terribly informative, not to her anyway. It contained Michelle Wong's name and a pair of phone numbers along with some Chinese characters written in a beautiful script. Since Charlotte couldn't read Chinese, the card was as mysterious as the woman in front of her. "I'll give this to him when I see him."

"Do you expect to see him soon?" Michelle asked.

"I've learned not to have too many expectations about the comings and goings around here," Charlotte said, knowing she was being difficult but finding she couldn't help it. There was something about the young woman that oozed arrogance, and Charlotte had been around enough people like that when she'd worked at Le Crabe Fou. She certainly wasn't going to cater to bad attitudes in her own inn, so she simply smiled at the woman and added, "It keeps me from stressing."

"I see," Michelle said. "I anticipate hearing from Jake soon, or I will return." Then she spun on her heel and walked out briskly, though

Charlotte suspected the young woman was suppressing the urge to stomp her feet.

Jolene grinned at Charlotte from the doorway. "I admire your style."

"Thank you," Charlotte said, but she wasn't entirely sure that Jolene's approval reflected well on her. She shouldn't have used that tone with the young businesswoman.

Jolene was still chuckling as she left the kitchen.

Charlotte turned back to the sink of dirty dishes and groaned. She went from cooking to cleaning up the kitchen, trying not to give in to her desire to ignore the dirty dishes.

A little later, the kitchen door swung open again to admit Jake and Paisley. Jake held a wrapped package, and Paisley cradled an antique tin box.

Charlotte recognized the tin box immediately. "I see you're both bearing gifts."

"Mom sent me over with the Christmas fudge," Paisley said. "She thought your guests would enjoy some."

"Are you sure?" Charlotte asked, though her mouth watered at the thought of her aunt's amazing fudge. Charlotte had never been able to capture the same flavor that Winnie seemed to get so effortlessly. "You have even more people at your house than we have here."

"We do," Paisley agreed. "But Mom can't eat it with her diabetes. And Maria and I talked about it and decided that it was a good idea to avoid filling our kids with sugar while they're trapped together. I'm not sure Mom and Dad's house would survive."

Charlotte laughed. "When you put it that way, it does make sense." She took the box from Paisley and set it down on the counter.

"Winnie told me to give this to Mom," Jake said. "It's a gift for Isaac."

"What is it?" Charlotte asked.

Jake shrugged. "She wouldn't tell me."

"You can put it under the tree, and I'll let your mom know." Charlotte gave him Michelle Wong's business card. "A woman in her early twenties stopped by earlier and insisted on speaking with you today."

Jake appeared startled, but he recovered quickly. "Thanks. I'd better go." He smiled at Charlotte and Paisley, then stuffed the business card into his pocket and rushed out of the room.

Paisley glanced around the kitchen. "Now tell me what I can do to help."

"Really?" Charlotte asked.

"Sure. I'm not needed at home, and it appears that I could be needed here. Besides, Mom told me I should help out."

Charlotte was surprised to feel her eyes burning and blinked before tears could form. Once again, she was massively grateful for her aunt's seemingly magical ability to know exactly what people needed.

21

Ivy

Ivy slumped into the luxurious leather seat of Holly's car and sighed. The smell of leather usually evoked comforting memories of Ivy's youth when she'd gone to horse camp, but today even that couldn't lift her spirits.

Ivy and Holly had spent the morning searching for Ballard. For a while Holly's boundless optimism had infected her, making her believe they'd be able to find him. The thought of talking to him, of risking face-to-face rejection, had been terrifying. But the slim chance that it would work out had buoyed her through the first two bed-and-breakfasts they'd visited. But it didn't take long for that optimism to drain from her again, leaving her more discouraged than ever.

None of the places on the list they'd gotten from Grace would comment on their guests. Not even in response to tears or trickery. Ivy had to admit that Holly was inventive about the trickery, moving smoothly from claiming to be Ballard's heartbroken wife to pretending to be his sister.

In the afternoon, Jolene had invited them to get a massage with her, but they declined. Instead, Ivy and Holly had driven to downtown Magnolia Harbor for lunch and shopping. Holly had thought that a leisurely afternoon in the charming town would make Ivy feel better, but it hadn't worked. Now they were returning to the inn, and Ivy couldn't wait to retreat to her room.

"We can't give up yet," Holly said. "We need some restful veranda gazing so we can regroup. Then we can surely come up with another plan."

"I think the plan should be to let Ballard live his life," Ivy responded. "And admit that I made my bed and now I should lie in it."

"Don't talk like that," Holly said firmly. "We haven't found him yet, but that doesn't mean we won't."

"He's probably not even in Magnolia Harbor anymore," Ivy muttered, slumping even more. "I'll bet he went home."

Holly glanced at her friend. "If you slide down any farther, you're going to be a puddle in the floorboards."

Ivy sighed deeply and dragged herself back up to a more normal sitting posture. "I feel like I belong in the floorboards, along with my heart."

"You give up entirely too easily," Holly chided. "If I did that, I would not be the managing editor at the magazine. When I come to a roadblock, I kick it until it backs down."

Ivy managed a smile. "That I can believe."

"Believe it and do it," Holly insisted. "You took some bad advice—bad for you anyway—and it led to some rotten results, but that doesn't have to be the end of the story."

"Not every story ends with the prince carrying the princess away," Ivy argued.

"I hope not," Holly said with a grunt. "Anyone who thinks I need to be carried instead of walking on my own two feet wouldn't be my prince for very long."

Ivy laughed. She could imagine Holly in some classic fairy tale giving a poor prince a hard time for thinking she needed to be rescued. She was positively giggling when she said, "I can picture you as Sleeping Beauty, punching the prince on the nose for waking you up when you were having a nice dream."

Holly tossed her head, making her curls bounce. "That sounds about right."

By the time they arrived at the Magnolia Harbor Inn, Ivy was laughing loudly as she envisioned Holly in a variety of classic princess stories and the unfortunate princes coming into contact with her.

Ivy related her thoughts to Holly, and her friend cheerfully agreed with each story variation, which made Ivy laugh even harder.

As they piled out of Holly's car, Ivy stood for a moment, taking a deep breath of the clean, cool air and letting her gaze sweep across the house and lawns. This was such a beautiful place, and she knew it should be a healing place, especially this time of year. But maybe her broken heart needed more than her best friends and the inn could provide.

"Come on," Holly said, pulling Ivy from her thoughts. "We'd better go face Jolene. She's probably not going to appreciate us sneaking out without her."

Ivy groaned. "Oh, good. Something else to dread."

Holly walked around the car and slung an arm around Ivy's shoulders. "It's okay. I'll protect you."

Ivy let Holly usher her toward the house. In her preoccupation, Ivy didn't immediately realize that someone was sitting in one of the chairs on the front veranda. When she did, she froze, making Holly stumble a bit from the sudden stop.

"What's the matter?" Holly asked.

"Ballard." Ivy's voice was barely a whisper.

"Huh?" Holly scanned the area, then spotted the man sitting on the veranda. "That's Ballard?"

Ivy couldn't find the voice to answer, so she simply nodded.

"Well, what are you waiting for?" Holly asked, nudging Ivy. "Go talk to him."

Ivy remained frozen. She couldn't believe that Ballard was here. He was staring straight out across the lawn and clearly hadn't seen them yet as their approach from the parking lot was at an angle. Ivy finally pulled herself free of the morass of shock and continued walking toward the mansion.

When they reached the veranda, Holly squeezed Ivy's arm, then kept walking right past Ballard and into the inn.

Ivy stopped at the top of the veranda steps. "Ballard?"

He jumped to his feet and faced her, shifting nervously. "I thought maybe you'd call me or text me after we talked, but you didn't. I thought maybe I should go home, but I couldn't. So I came here. It was the only place I wanted to be. The place where you were."

Once again, Ivy couldn't find any words, so she just nodded.

"You told me where you were staying," he said, a trace of defensiveness in his voice. "I wasn't sure if you'd think it was creepy that I came over, but we need to talk. Am I wrong?"

"No, you're not wrong." Ivy could hear the pain in her own voice and hated it. She sounded like a lost child. She longed for the kind of strength that Holly and Jolene showed all the time, but she wasn't that person. She never had been.

"Would you be willing to have dinner with me?" he asked, his gaze intense. "We could talk."

"I'd love that," she said honestly.

Ballard smiled.

Ivy felt something unfold in her chest, as if her heart had been a tight fist that now relaxed.

"I hear good things about The Tidewater across the lake."

"It's wonderful," she said. "I'm sorry you got turned away from the comedy show."

"I didn't have a reservation," Ballard said. "But I have one now."

"You do?" Ivy asked, surprised.

He nodded. "I figured if you were willing to have dinner with me, I wanted to take you somewhere nice. You should always go to nice places."

There he was again, insisting she was better than she was. "When is the reservation?"

"In an hour," Ballard answered.

Ivy gasped. "I should get dressed right now. Do you mind waiting?"

His smile never wavered, though his eyes grew serious. "I'd wait for you forever."

"I'll be right back," Ivy said with a voice roughened by sudden unshed tears. She rushed past him and up the stairs.

Before Ivy could make it to her suite, Jolene burst out of her room.

Holly followed and put her hand on Jolene's arm, obviously attempting to stop her.

Jolene shrugged off Holly's hand and gaped at Ivy. "What are you doing?"

"Getting ready to change my clothes," Ivy said, walking past her friends and opening her door. Unfortunately she couldn't step through and close the door in Jolene's face. She wasn't that bold yet. As a result, Jolene and Holly followed her into the room.

"Have you lost your mind?" Jolene asked. "I thought you'd learned your lesson about the pain and drama of serious relationships. But then I find out Holly was helping you search for the guy so you could beg him to come back to you. A guy who stepped out on you with someone else."

"I don't have time to discuss this," Ivy said. "I have to change." She opened her wardrobe and scanned the clothes.

"Just tell me why," Jolene said.

"Because being without Ballard makes me miserable, and it apparently makes him miserable to be without me." Ivy took her new periwinkle dress from the wardrobe. She'd almost forgotten about it.

Jolene crossed her arms and frowned at the dress in Ivy's hands. "You shouldn't waste that dress. It's for something special."

"Then it will be perfect for tonight," Ivy said.

Jolene snorted. "What you described isn't love. It's mental illness. You're only going to make yourself more miserable. You need to wake up and get back to following the plan."

"No, *you* need to wake up," Holly said, stepping between Jolene and Ivy. "And realize that your plan might be best for you, but it's not right for everyone."

"What are you talking about?" Jolene asked, putting her hands on her hips. "It's worked for you too."

While her friends debated, Ivy quietly slipped into the dress. She wasn't going to let anything keep her from getting back downstairs in time, and she was immensely grateful to Holly for keeping Jolene distracted.

"I've always kept my options open," Holly said. "I love my job and my life, but I don't reject the idea of adding a relationship."

"It doesn't work that way," Jolene snapped. "I've seen it again and again. As soon as you let a man into your life, the things that belong to you disappear. You stop being yourself."

"And I've seen again and again that it doesn't have to be that way," Holly said. "You see what you want to see because it makes your life choices easier, and I respect that for you. But Ivy and I aren't made that way. Ivy has already found the change she wants, and I'm open to change as well, if that's what the Lord has in store for me."

Jolene narrowed her eyes. "You haven't fallen for that quiet soldier, have you?"

The question caught Ivy's attention, and she turned to watch Holly's reaction.

"No, I haven't done any falling," Holly said. "But my life is never too full for someone new."

Jolene shook her head. "I don't understand why you two want that kind of chaos and heartache in your lives."

"Whoa," Holly said, laughing. "I never said I'm up for chaos and heartache. But I am thinking Isaac is going to be a good friend. Friends are important relationships too, aren't they?"

"Yeah, friends are important," Jolene said with a sigh. "Honestly, I want to be the best friend I can be to each of you. Even when I think you're nutty. As your friend, it's my duty to tell you. But it's also my duty to support you when you think you've found happiness."

Holly smiled. "That's right. And for the record, we think you're nutty too."

"But the best kind of nutty," Ivy clarified.

"I guess that leaves us with one thing to do." Jolene threw open her arms. "Group hug."

They all huddled for a moment, and Ivy found the warmth of that acceptance melted away a lot of the pain she'd carried with her to the inn. "I appreciate you guys so much."

"Ditto," Jolene said as she released them. "Listen, you two do whatever is right for you. I'm always going to back you up. And if it all crashes and burns, I'll be there with some sad movies and lots of chocolate."

"I'll bet you'll say that you told us so," Holly added with a grin.

"Until I'm hoarse," Jolene admitted. "I'm still me."

"That's okay. We knew who you were from the start," Ivy said. "Now, if you guys don't mind, I need to fix my makeup and brush my hair. I have a dinner reservation."

"Well, at least he made a reservation," Jolene said approvingly. She turned to Holly. "You want to go see if there are any appetizers out yet?"

"You go ahead," Holly said. "I need to make a few phone calls. But if I don't get down in time for social hour, I'll catch you for dinner. Okay?"

"Fine," Jolene huffed. "But let's not lose all our friend time while we're here."

"We won't," Ivy said. "Now get out."

They all laughed.

After one more group hug, Ivy managed to push them out the door. Once it was closed, she leaned against it, taking a few deep breaths. Now all she had to do was get through dinner. That should be easy, right?

Grace

As Grace made her bed, she hummed under her breath. It was Christmas Eve, and that meant she'd be busy every minute, but she didn't mind. Helping to create a wonderful holiday event for family and friends was the best kind of busy.

She gently smoothed the cozy quilted coverlet as she went through her mental list of people who would be at the party. Her family, the inn's guests, and Dean. Grace smiled briefly as his eager face popped into her head. She hoped the gift he'd come up with would be a hit with her sister.

Grace straightened and surveyed the bedroom. Her usual decor was mostly white with accents in pale taupe. Charlotte had teased her about it looking like the inside of an eggshell, but Grace normally found the lack of bright colors soothing. Christmas had inspired her to add a dash of holiday style even to her quiet quarters. She had hung white lights around her bed for a bit of sparkle and added some Christmas pillows in muted shades of red and green.

Winston whined and plopped down at her feet.

"Are you ready for breakfast?" Grace asked the dog.

He ran to the door.

"I'll take that as a yes." Grace grinned as she followed him.

Winston led the way to the kitchen, glancing back at her to make sure she was coming.

As Grace had expected, Charlotte was already up to her elbows in cooking. The kitchen was filled with an aroma that was a mixture of bacon and something sweet. As Grace approached the counter, she saw Charlotte expertly cutting up fruit and dumping it into a bowl.

"Good morning," Charlotte said.

"Morning." Grace put kibble in Winston's bowl and refreshed his water. After she washed her hands, she asked her sister, "What can I do?"

"Here." Charlotte pushed a loaf of bread and a cookie cutter toward Grace. "We're going to have egg-in-the-hole. I made this rosemary and pepper bread yesterday exactly for this. Cut thick slices and butter both sides of each slice, then make a hole in the middle. I'll use the bread as a frame for fried eggs and grill the bread at the same time."

"Sounds tasty." Grace took the bread knife from the knife block and began slicing. She was careful to make her slices uniform since she knew how Charlotte could spot any irregularity.

"I'm also broiling bacon with a maple and brown sugar glaze." Charlotte tapped the edge of the bowl in front of her. "And we're having a nice mixed fruit salad with mint. I thought I'd use up all the fruit left over from social hour. I made orange scones for anyone who doesn't want bacon and eggs for breakfast."

"It's a good thing Winnie isn't having breakfast with us," Grace remarked. "None of that would be on her diabetic diet."

"Yeah, I'll admit I'm taking advantage of the fact that all our guests are young with speedy metabolisms."

Charlotte's comment about speedy metabolisms reminded Grace of Jake. "Did you see Jake yesterday? He'd already come and gone by the time I got home, and I wanted to ask him for gift suggestions for Isaac. I still haven't found a gift for him."

"Yes, I saw him come home," Charlotte said, then smiled. "And you're in luck because he brought something from Winnie for Isaac."

"That's a relief." Grace paused in buttering the first slice of bread. "But what did Winnie send for Isaac?"

"I have no idea," Charlotte said. "It was already wrapped. And she hadn't told Jake either. I told him to put it under the tree. After that, I suppose he could have gone searching for his visitor."

"Visitor?" Grace was still frozen with a slice of bread in one hand and a butter knife in the other. "What visitor? How come you didn't tell me any of this after I got home yesterday?"

"I was in the zone," Charlotte said. "I had hors d'oeuvres to finish and today's party to prep for. If Paisley hadn't come by to help, I'd have been swamped." She pointed at the slice of bread in Grace's hand. "Butter!"

Grace obediently slathered the bread slices, but her mind was elsewhere. "I didn't know Paisley came by." Then she frowned at Charlotte. "But as I remember, you told me it was okay to go shopping."

"I was being brave." Charlotte pointed at the bread again. "Butter faster."

"Fine." Grace continued buttering the bread. "Tell me about Jake's visitor."

"She didn't stay long," Charlotte said as she squeezed a lemon over the cut-up fruit in the bowl.

"She?" Grace's hands froze once more, but she quickly returned to buttering before her sister could give her orders again.

"Yep." Charlotte picked a few mint leaves from a small plant in a colorful ceramic pot and began tearing them up and dropping them into the fruit salad. "She was in her early twenties. Very pretty. Her name is Michelle Wong. She left a business card, and I gave it to Jake when he came home."

"Did he seem pleased?" Grace asked as she switched from buttering the bread to cutting holes with the cookie cutter. "Like she could have been his girlfriend?"

Charlotte paused and wrinkled her nose. "Judging from her attitude and his, I don't think so. He actually seemed a little annoyed, but he wouldn't talk about it. He only thanked me and shoved her business card into his pocket."

"I'm not sure how hard you tried to get him to talk."

"I was working."

"Precisely." Grace set aside the cutter and moved all the bread to a plate. "I wish I'd been here."

Charlotte rolled her eyes, but before she could respond, a timer went off. "Could you pull the bacon from the oven, please?" she asked sweetly.

Grace sighed and took out the broiler pan full of bacon that glistened in its sugar glaze. She had to admit it looked delicious. She set the pan on top of the stove.

"I really don't think the woman was Jake's girlfriend," Charlotte said. "She was all business, and when she found out Jake wasn't here, she didn't want to hang around."

"Maybe she'll come back," Grace suggested.

Charlotte walked over to remove the bacon from the pan. "Maybe."

"I'll go set the table for breakfast." Before Grace left the kitchen, she turned to her sister. "Thanks for handling everything yesterday."

Charlotte smiled. "We're in this together."

"Always," Grace agreed.

When breakfast was ready, Grace was surprised to see Ivy was the first to arrive. Not only that, but the normally distressed young woman was positively radiant. If anything, Ivy's face lit up more as she caught sight of Grace. She hurried over to her.

"Good morning," Grace said. "Merry Christmas Eve."

Ivy laughed. "Merry Christmas Eve to you too. Breakfast smells wonderful. The food here has been amazing."

Grace refrained from mentioning that Ivy had barely eaten any of it, but she was gratified to see the young woman cheerfully fill a plate.

Ivy glanced at Grace, her expression suddenly shy. "I don't know the protocol for the party tonight. Is it all right if I bring someone?"

"Well, the theme is family and friends," Grace said, smiling. "As inn guests, you're all friends. Is your guest one of your family or friends?"

"A friend," Ivy admitted. "And maybe family someday." Her cheeks became a lovely shade of pink.

"In that case, it sounds as if your friend would be a perfect addition to the party tonight," Grace said. "It's Christmas. We should be with the people who make us happy."

"Oh good. Thank you." Ivy ducked her head, clearly trying to hide her blush.

Grace wanted to quiz her guest further, but she didn't want to cause her any more embarrassment. She busied herself by arranging napkins into a fan.

Jolene and Holly walked into the dining room together. Neither glowed like Ivy, but they perked up when they saw their friend.

Ivy waved at them and sat down with her full plate.

"You came in so late," Jolene teased as she sat beside Ivy. "And so quietly. You didn't get to tell us about your date."

"It was good," Ivy answered.

"Good?" Holly echoed, sitting down across from Ivy. "You're lit up like the star on a Christmas tree. I'd say it was better than good."

Though she stood away from the trio, Grace watched Ivy's face carefully. She was concerned that the teasing might hurt Ivy's feelings. And Grace didn't want to see anything dull the happiness on Ivy's face. But it was soon clear that wasn't going to happen.

"It was wonderful." Ivy beamed, and it warmed Grace's heart. "We were honest with each other for the first time. We talked about everything. About what we wanted from life. About how we felt."

"You're blushing," Jolene observed. "What else happened?"

"We said we love each other." Ivy's blush only highlighted the joy shining in her eyes. "Ballard said he loves me. We both decided together not to go too fast, but we're definitely together, really for the first time, since now we're both being truly honest."

"Honesty is always the way to go," Holly said.

Jolene shrugged. "Except when sneakiness is more exciting."

Holly and Ivy groaned in unison.

"You're never going to change, are you?" Holly asked.

"I'm not planning on it," Jolene said blithely. "But I'll let you guys change all you want, and I'll still love you. That's all I can promise."

"That's enough for me," Ivy said. "So how was your evening?"

"We spent it without a date," Jolene grumbled, "which is why we want to live vicariously through you." She put an arm around Ivy. "Tell us more."

"Leave out nothing," Holly agreed, leaning forward. "We want details. What did you eat? Did he open the car door for you? Was there kissing? Was it good?"

"Let's see." Ivy counted off on her fingers as she answered. "I had seafood, and Ballard had steak. I think he would have opened the door for me, but I was nervous and opened it first." She paused, blushing again. "Yes, on the kissing, but I am not telling you about it."

"Spoilsport," Jolene said with a laugh. "You know we'll get the rest of the details out of you eventually."

To Grace's surprise, Ivy smiled and shook her head, her expression still dreamy with joy.

Confident that Christmas Eve was going well so far, Grace bustled off to the kitchen, hopeful that Jake would soon be downstairs. She definitely had questions for him.

23

Jake

Jake crept down the back stairs, his soft-soled shoes making almost no noise on the wooden steps. He felt a little ridiculous. A twenty-four-year-old man should not be hiding from his mother, but here he was doing just that. He suspected Charlotte had told his mom about Michelle Wong, and that was going to produce questions Jake didn't want to answer. At least not yet.

He could have gone down the front stairs and bypassed the kitchen, but then he wouldn't be able to pretend that he wasn't trying to duck his mom and aunt. It would only lead to more questions, and when the Christmas party rolled around, he'd be stuck.

I'll have made a decision by then. Hopefully.

As Jake neared the bottom of the staircase, he took a deep breath and raced down the last few steps. Using the back stairs sent him into the kitchen, but he strode across the room and pretended not to notice the startled looks of his mom and aunt. "Good morning," he called out, then winced inwardly and dialed back the cheer a little.

"We need to have a chat," his mother said.

"Sure," he said as he reached around her and snagged a scone from a rack on the counter. "But I need to run to the store. Can we talk when I get back?" He took a big bite of scone, hoping the food in his mouth would keep his mother from expecting conversation.

"What do you need to go to the store for?" Mom asked suspiciously.

Jake pointed at his full mouth as he chewed.

But his mother merely tilted her head, giving him a level stare. Clearly she intended to wait.

After nearly choking himself swallowing the huge bite, Jake managed to say, "You're not supposed to ask those kinds of questions on Christmas Eve." He gave her a peck on the cheek. "You'll have to wait until we open presents tonight."

Mom didn't move out of his way. Instead, she folded her arms over her chest. "So you're off to buy me a present. Aren't you running a little late?"

Jake smiled right into her suspicious blue eyes. "And that's why I can't hang around and chat."

"Did you get a chance to talk to Michelle Wong?" Charlotte asked, her tone a little too nonchalant.

Jake shot her an annoyed glance. "Not yet. But I'm sure I will." He started to step around his mother.

But she shifted position so that he'd actually have to move her if he wanted to escape. "And who is Michelle Wong? Are you dating this woman?"

Jake considered lying. If he said Michelle Wong was his ex, then his mom would probably let it all go. He had no idea who the woman was, though he assumed she came from the company who'd been barraging him with messages. From the description Charlotte had given him yesterday, Michelle was the right age to be his pretend ex. Still, lying to his mom? On Christmas?

Against his better judgment, he blurted, "Not anymore." As soon as the words were out of his mouth, the lie seemed to lodge uncomfortably into his stomach next to the wad of scone.

From the corner of his eye, he saw the skeptical expression on his aunt's face. She wasn't buying it.

On the other hand, his mom settled down considerably. She

dropped her hands to her sides. "Well, that explains the need for another present. But you shouldn't give her a gift if you don't intend to get back together with her. It may seem nice, but it's going to send the wrong message."

"Yeah, you're right, but I still have to go to the store." Jake ducked around his mom while she was still a little confused and made it to the door without further obstruction. "We'll talk when I get back."

When Jake made it to the front veranda, he stopped and leaned on one of the columns and groaned. He couldn't believe he'd lied to his mother. He was a terrible person. Should he have talked to her about the job offer? But he still didn't know what he planned to do, not even with his great-aunt's wise advice or Maria's quirky suggestion. He couldn't handle any more well-meaning family input. The idea made his head spin.

He hurried down the veranda steps and headed for his car, slipping the rest of the scone into the pocket of his jacket. It felt good to drive away from the inn. He loved the place normally, especially at the holidays. And Magnolia Harbor was so warm and welcoming. He had become a city boy in the last few years, but Magnolia Harbor was special.

With no actual shopping needed, Jake drove aimlessly for a while, trying to sort out his dilemma. Finally, he pulled into a convenience store. He had rushed out of the inn without a cup of coffee, and he was going to need one if he was to finish the breakfast in his pocket.

When Jake got out of the car and walked to the store, he noticed the windows were trimmed in slightly tattered silver tinsel. Inside, he wove between closely packed displays and shelving to reach the coffee dispenser. He filled the cup, then turned to the next counter to add cream to the coffee. That was when he spotted a metal rack labeled *Christmas Joy*. It was filled with what Jake assumed were gift possibilities.

After Jake snapped the lid on his coffee, he walked closer to examine all the Christmas joys on the rack. The items had been heavily picked over, which made Jake feel a bit sad. Who shopped for Christmas gifts at a convenience store? Still, a few things sat on the top shelf. He tapped the top of a bobblehead Santa dressed in a grass skirt. Santa nodded enthusiastically as he bobbled at the hips as well. The overall combination was more than a little disturbing.

Next to the Santa was a stuffed reindeer that stared at Jake through a pair of mismatched eyes. One of the eyes was set a good quarter inch lower than the other, giving the poor reindeer an expression of perpetual confusion.

The third thing on the shelf was a rubbery fish mounted on a faux wooden plaque and adorned with a tiny Santa hat. A small sticker promised the fish would sing if you pushed the red button on the plaque. Jake decided not to push the button.

He took a long sip of his coffee as he exchanged looks with the wonky reindeer again. Who would possibly want such a confused creature? For reasons Jake couldn't possibly have explained, he gave in to a rogue impulse and grabbed the reindeer, carrying it to the register to pay for it along with the cup of coffee.

Back in the car, he set the reindeer on the seat beside him. "I think I may be losing my mind," he told it.

If the reindeer had an opinion on that remark, he kept it to himself.

After some more aimless driving, Jake stopped at a small park to eat his scone and drink the rest of his coffee.

He sat on the edge of a picnic table and gazed across the meadows of the quiet park. Was his reluctance to take the job in China simply a fear of trying something new? Or did he truly love his job and his present life too much to give them up? Jake wondered if he was being honest with himself. There were so many possibilities, and he wasn't sure what was going on in his own heart.

Soon his scone was gone and his cup was empty, and he had no reason to stay away from the inn any longer. He should probably be helping with the party preparations anyway. He knew he'd been woefully self-absorbed since coming home, and he hoped he hadn't hurt his mom's feelings. *I can't believe I lied to her.* That reminder made him feel sick again.

Finally, he brushed the crumbs from his jeans and tossed his coffee cup in one of the wire trash cans on the way to the car. It was time to face the music.

When Jake arrived at the inn, he didn't immediately pay attention to the woman standing on the front veranda. After all, three of the inn's guests were young women. But when he headed up the path to the front steps with the wonky reindeer tucked under his arm, he realized that the woman watching him approach was definitely Chinese and none of the guests were Asian.

Jake smiled at the scowling woman. "Michelle Wong, I assume?"

She nodded. "We have put a great deal of effort into trying to get in contact with you."

"I know, and I'm sorry." Jake stopped for a moment at the bottom of the steps but found he didn't enjoy having the woman scowling down at him. So he climbed the steps to stand beside her. "I haven't made up my mind, and I didn't see any point in further discussion until I had."

"But further discussion would allow us to assuage your doubts," Michelle said. "I have been authorized to raise our original offer substantially."

"Why?" Jake asked. He didn't understand why this company was so interested in hiring him. He was a good programmer, but there were a lot of other good programmers.

"If you have been reading the e-mails the company has sent, you would know that we have carefully researched your part in the lucrative and wildly popular Gift Assistant. It was your idea originally. You found something people needed without even knowing they needed it. That is the kind of thinking we want for our company."

"It's a truly flattering offer," Jake said. "But I'm still not ready to decide."

Michelle's face darkened, and she actually stamped her foot. "I have come a long way to get your answer. I'm missing my own Christmas to be here."

"I didn't ask you to come and certainly not all the way from China," Jake said mildly, though he had to admit that he did feel a bit guilty about making anyone miss their Christmas.

"I didn't say you did," she snapped. "And I didn't actually come from China. I'm tied to a branch office in California. Still, since I have to be here, the least you can do is give me an answer."

"I'm sorry, but I can't give you what I don't have," he said.

Her eyes began to shine, and she turned away from him. "All right," Michelle said, her voice slightly roughened. "I will be in town until you decide. Please call the number on the card I left." She gave him a sideways glance. "You do have the card, don't you?"

"Yes," he said. Guilt nudged him. "I am sorry about your Christmas. My mom and aunt are hosting a party here this evening. It's for family, but it also includes all the inn guests, so it's not only family. Would you like to come?"

She faced him again. "Will you have the answer to my question?"

"I don't know," Jake admitted. "I'll try. But we'll have really good food and probably some fun too."

Michelle frowned. "I'm not good at fun."

"Then you can just eat the food and watch the fun."

She pointed a manicured nail at the stuffed animal under Jake's arm. "What is that?"

Jake had forgotten about the toy. He pulled it out and peered into its wonky face again. "It's a reindeer. I saw it at a convenience store and felt sorry for it. It's a little goofy."

Michelle smile slightly. "It reminds me of you."

He laughed in surprise. "Ouch, I think. So I look goofy?"

"You look like you are having trouble with a decision." Then her smile slipped away. "And you need to overcome that. Today. It's already too late for me to get home for Christmas, but if you make the right decision, at least I can give my bosses the gift they're hoping for." And with that she marched past him and down the steps.

Jake watched Michelle until she was out of sight, then realized she hadn't actually said whether she was coming to the party. Just in case Michelle showed up, he'd better tell his aunt there might be an extra guest.

But at the moment, he didn't have the energy to face his aunt or his mom, so he detoured up the front stairs and made it to his room without running into anyone. He tossed the reindeer on the bed and unloaded the loose change from his pocket onto one of the nightstands. He hated the sound of change jingling as he walked.

Jake sat down heavily in one of the chairs. He'd set himself a deadline, and he had to have a decision by the party this evening. But what was the right call? Go or stay?

As he pondered the question, his gaze rested on the pile of change on the nightstand, and he thought about what his cousin had said. Did he dare flip a coin for such a momentous decision?

He shrugged. It couldn't be any worse than sitting here with no idea what to do.

Jake crossed the room in three steps, grabbed a quarter, and rested it on his bent thumb. "If it's heads, I stay with the company and the job I have," he said, feeling absurd saying the words aloud. "If it's tails, I go to China and a new adventure."

Holding his breath, he flipped the coin. The metal caught the light as it spun in the air. Jake tried to catch it but missed it by a hair. The quarter landed on the thick blue duvet cover.

Jake stared down at the coin and then laughed. Maria was right. He knew exactly what to do.

He pulled Michelle's business card from his pocket and picked up his phone.

Grace

Grace ducked to one side as Sam and Monica speed-walked by, and she nearly laughed aloud. The children knew better than to run in the house, but they pushed walking to the very edge.

It reminded her of the ways Jake would find loopholes in the rules when he was a little boy. *I suppose Charlotte and I did that too.* Though Grace couldn't come up with specific examples. Since she was thirteen years older than Charlotte, they hadn't been coconspirators in a lot of mischief. Then she smiled. *Maybe a little trouble.*

Grace walked to the living room and stood inside the doorway to bask in the glow of the joy in front of her. Christmas music played quietly, but she couldn't make out the song over the laughter and chatter of the people assembled there.

Jake sat on a sofa beside Michelle Wong. The young woman wore a business suit as if she lived in them, though she also had Winston sprawled on her lap. Jake was showing Michelle something on his phone. She smiled at him, but Grace noticed there was no spark there. They weren't dating. Jake hadn't been honest about Michelle when Grace had asked about her earlier. So what was Michelle doing here?

Grace forced her attention away from her son and noticed Winnie sitting by the fireplace with her daughter Maria. Winnie wore a three-button blazer with a scalloped front edge. It was the perfect balance of polished and feminine and suited her well.

Nearby Ricky and Sarah were playing a board game with their

cousins Sam and Monica, much to Grace's delight. Maria's husband, Adam, traded corny jokes with Paisley's husband, Bryson, while Paisley rolled her eyes and pretended not to be amused.

Grace saw the inn guests seemed to be enjoying themselves as well. Isaac was chatting with Gus, their heads together so they could hear each other over the general uproar in the room. Ivy, Holly, and Jolene sat on the other sofa, talking and laughing.

Grace couldn't help but smile at the man who sat wedged in the corner of the long sofa with the three women. Ballard held Ivy's hand and seemed completely content to be slightly squashed. Grace wondered if the man was aware that he wore a slight smile, and she suspected that Ivy had been right when she'd admitted that Ballard was a friend who might become family someday. Grace could definitely imagine the couple's friendship growing into something far more permanent.

Ballard whispered something in Ivy's ear. Whatever he said, it made the young woman blush, though her expression was nothing short of joyous.

A number of empty glasses and dessert plates were scattered around the room, so Grace picked up a tray from one of the side tables and began gathering the dirty dishes. Soon the tray was full.

As Grace was sorting out how to fit two more glasses onto the tray, Paisley walked over and took the tray. "Let me help," she said. "It's the least I can do after you and Charlotte have done so much."

"Thank you." Grace picked up the extra glasses and walked companionably with her cousin. "How are you enjoying your holiday break so far?"

Paisley sighed. "Well, I do have to work on some lesson plans over break, but of course I'm not doing that today. Right now I'm simply enjoying the party. Which reminds me, both of my children want to know when we're opening presents."

"So the children were wondering about the gifts." Grace laughed. "As I recall, you never wanted to put off the gift exchange either."

"Guilty as charged," Paisley said with a grin.

"We'll start as soon as I can drag Charlotte from the kitchen," Grace assured her.

"Considering how handsome her kitchen help is, that could take some effort," Paisley said.

When Grace and Paisley entered the kitchen, Charlotte and Dean were arguing about whether he had tasted rosemary in the stuffing.

"Forget it," Charlotte said, waving a damp wooden spoon at him. "I'm not helping you reverse engineer the secret family stuffing recipe."

"Hey, what about the spirit of giving?" Dean turned to Grace and Paisley, his hands outspread. "What do you say, ladies? You ate the stuffing too. Was it rosemary?"

"Sorry, but my name's Paisley, not Rosemary," she quipped as she began unloading the tray of dirty dishes onto the counter.

Grace and Charlotte laughed at their cousin's joke.

"I don't think you're going to find anyone in the family willing to give up the secret, not even for the holiday," Grace told Dean. "But on another topic, apparently the children are clamoring for the gift exchange. Can you two join us?"

"Go ahead and start," Charlotte responded. "We'll be along as soon as we're done in here."

"Sounds good," Paisley said and rushed out the door.

Grace chuckled. "I knew it wasn't only the children who were in a hurry to open presents."

"Some things never change," Charlotte said as she pulled another dish from the dishwasher and began drying it.

"Your stubbornness, for example," Dean said. "Surely you can at least verify the rosemary."

Grace shook her head and left them to their happy arguing. As she walked into the living room, she was amused to find Paisley already announcing the gift exchange. Opening presents was far from a quick process. Gifts were stacked all around the tree, and Paisley appointed her children and the teenagers as Santa's elves to deliver presents to their recipients.

Sam and Monica struggled a bit to read some of the names on the tags, especially the ones written in cursive, but everyone was patient. Grace thought they enjoyed the children's enthusiasm as much as she did.

Grace's attention was pulled to the love seat as Ricky handed a gift bag to Michelle.

"A gift?" Michelle asked, the surprise in her voice sounding almost like wonder.

Grace watched Jake, intensely curious about what he'd bought for Michelle.

Jake avoided his mom's gaze. Instead, he gestured at the bag and said, "Be careful. He's a wild one."

Michelle pulled a silly-looking stuffed reindeer out of the bag. Its eyes weren't even level.

Grace felt an immediate rush of dismay. What was Jake thinking? That couldn't be something the young woman would enjoy, but to her surprise, Michelle laughed and hugged the reindeer.

I guess I don't know everything about people, Grace thought ruefully. *Thanks for always keeping me from getting a big head, Lord.*

25

Ivy

When Ivy, Jolene, and Holly were presented with identical packages, all three women gasped.

"If these gifts didn't look the same, I'd be afraid to open mine," Ivy said, glancing at Jolene. "I can easily imagine a pillowcase with the plan embroidered on it."

Holly shook her head. "Don't give her any ideas."

Ivy laughed.

"I'm a little surprised you managed to get me a present," Holly told Ivy. "We all know your first shopping trip was a ruse to hunt for you-know-who."

Ivy smiled, then turned to Ballard.

He positively beamed at Holly's words. He'd been holding Ivy's hand ever since they'd sat down on the sofa. Now he squeezed it gently.

"I remembered this particular present from my perfectly valid window-shopping trip," Ivy explained. "So I stopped by the shop last night, and they did the gift wrap." She smiled. "I was hardly going to let you go without a gift today of all days."

"Well, I got yours yesterday evening," Jolene insisted, hugging her own present close. "After you'd snuck off to dinner. But I don't know when Holly got this one for me."

"Same time," Holly said. "And I think maybe the same place and the same gift-wrapping service."

When they opened the packages, they burst into laughter, then gushed over the scarves inside. Though technically they had all gotten the same gift, the three scarves were completely different in color and design.

Ivy was amused and charmed by the fact that they'd given one another the same gift while being unique. She realized the gesture fit them, since the three friends were uniquely different but somehow found a way to respect their differences and hang on to their friendship. Ivy knew that wasn't always easy to do, and she was grateful they had made it work.

"Isn't it lovely?" Ivy held out her thick burgundy scarf to show Ballard.

Jolene squealed over her emerald silk scarf with delicate embroidery in metallic gold. When she wrapped it around her neck, it made her red hair glow like a flame. "I love it." She gave Holly a huge hug.

Ivy wrapped the scarf around her neck and hugged Jolene. "Thank you for knowing I'd prefer cozy over bold."

"Cozy suits you. I thought this might feel like a hug from me when I can't be there to give you one in person," Jolene said gently. "Besides, it's red, like my hair."

Holly promptly wrapped her brightly patterned batik scarf around her waist to make a saucy belt on her creamy linen dress. "And I'm going to wear this a lot. Thanks so much, Ivy."

"You're welcome," Ivy said, embracing Holly.

Ballard tugged on the end of the scarf and whispered, "You look beautiful."

At the compliment, Ivy ducked her head. When she glanced up and gazed into Ballard's eyes, she saw so much warmth there that she almost gasped.

"Merry Christmas." Ballard smiled and put his arm around her.

"Merry Christmas," Ivy echoed. She still couldn't believe that Ballard was sitting here beside her in this spectacular inn on Christmas Eve. It felt like a dream. One that she hoped would never end.

26

Isaac

Isaac sat back and watched the others opening their Christmas presents. He chuckled when he noticed that Holly and her friends had exchanged the same gifts.

It was a surprise when Grace handed him a wrapped package. He had no idea what it could be or even who it was from. Isaac glanced down at the tag and saw that it was from Winnie. He scanned the room and met her eyes.

Winnie rose from her seat and walked over to Isaac. "I hope you like it."

"Thank you. I certainly wasn't expecting anything, so this is already a wonderful surprise." Isaac unwrapped the gift. Inside was a well-made but slightly scuffed case. He opened it to reveal a set of tools for an electrician.

"Do you do electrical work in the military?" Grace asked.

"Yes," Isaac said quietly as he ran a finger over the tools in his lap. "Before I joined up, I worked with an electrician who had this exact set. He taught me so much."

"That's wonderful," Grace said.

Isaac stared at the tools. He couldn't believe that Winnie had given him such an incredible gift. "Thank you. I don't know what else to say. This means so much."

"You're welcome," she replied and patted his hand.

Isaac smiled at Winnie and Grace. "I think everyone here may be angels sent to tell me something."

Winnie chuckled gently. "We're not angels, but maybe God is trying to help you with a decision."

"I have something for you too." Holly got up and came over to Isaac. She handed him a piece of paper. "Think of it as a theme gift."

Isaac scanned the paper. A name and phone number were written on it. "I'm not sure what this is for," he admitted. "Or who this person is."

"It's the name and number of an electrician I know in Atlanta." Holly ducked her head, making her dangling earrings catch the light. "Actually, he's my uncle. He always complains about how no one seems to want to work in the trades. If you want a job, he'll hire you. I already called and asked him about it."

Isaac was overwhelmed. He didn't trust himself to speak so he remained silent, his gaze on the tools.

"I'm not trying to tell you what you should do," Holly added, her tone slightly nervous. "I know it's still a tough decision. But don't make it because you think you have only one choice. Make it because you've found the best choice for you."

Isaac considered her words. "I will," he said.

As if recognizing that Isaac needed the attention pulled away from him, Paisley clapped. "Isn't it time someone found my present? Come on, guys!"

Isaac was grateful for the commotion as the children rushed over to the tree, laughing while they hunted for the gift with Paisley's name on it.

Holly sat down beside him. "Are you all right?"

"Yes," Isaac said, then cleared his throat. "I want to thank you for talking to your uncle about me. I can't tell you how much I appreciate it."

"It was my pleasure," she answered. "I know I said that I'm not trying to tell you what to do, but I hope you call him."

Isaac laughed. "Don't worry. I'm already planning on it." Lately he had been leaning in this direction, and he couldn't let such an amazing opportunity slip away.

"I'm happy to hear it," Holly said with a smile. "I hope we can keep in touch."

Isaac returned her smile. "Me too."

As Isaac and Holly talked about their favorite places in Atlanta, he almost shook his head in wonder. Even though this trip to Magnolia Harbor hadn't turned out the way he'd expected, it had turned out better than he'd ever imagined.

Isaac couldn't wait to go home and begin his new life.

Charlotte

Charlotte set aside the last of the clean dishes while Dean loaded the dishwasher. She saw that he wasn't putting the glasses in exactly as she would have, and she bit her lip to avoid telling him. It was Christmas, and she really should cut him some slack. She grinned. Not much, of course, but some. He'd helped a lot with the last-minute details and with serving.

"What?" Dean asked.

"What what?" As soon as the words were out of her mouth, Charlotte felt a little silly. How did Dean manage to bring out the grumpy teenager in her?

"You were grinning," he answered. "What's so funny?"

"I was thinking that I appreciate how much you helped today," she said. "But then I got over it."

Dean laughed. "Good. I wouldn't know what to do with you if you got all mushy at Christmas." His expression turned serious. "I enjoyed the dinner. It was fantastic."

Charlotte smiled. She liked hearing Dean compliment her because she knew he was sincere.

Dean turned to lean against the counter, his arms crossed. "Want to go watch everyone opening their gifts?"

"I thought you'd probably find that dull," Charlotte said. "Seeing a bunch of people you hardly know get presents."

Dean straightened up. "Hey, I'm a people person. I love seeing others happy."

"Fine, let's go watch the festivities." As they walked to the living room, Charlotte paused to reach for an empty glass left on a table in the hallway.

But Dean caught her wrist. "Leave it. If you pause at every empty glass, we'll miss all the presents."

She glanced at him. His sudden interest in the gifts was suspicious. She wondered if he was expecting a present. She did have a small gift for him, but he shouldn't assume that he'd get something. She didn't appreciate the idea of being predictable.

Monica burst from the living room and ran right into Charlotte, bouncing off her so hard that Dean had to grab the girl's arm to keep her from falling.

"Running in the house?" Charlotte said. "Best not let your mom see that."

"It was Mom who told me to get you," Monica replied. "She said that you've missed almost all the gifts. And if you don't come now, she's taking your presents." She frowned. "I told her it's not nice to take other people's presents, and Grandma agreed with me."

Charlotte was sure Winnie would agree with that. Though not at all straitlaced, her aunt was definitely a defender of rights. "Well, we're coming now," she said.

When they walked into the room, Charlotte took in the chaotic and joyful scene. Everyone seemed to be having a wonderful time. She grinned when she saw Winston reveling in the attention Michelle was giving him. When Michelle had arrived for the party, Charlotte had apologized for her earlier behavior, and Michelle had apologized to her as well.

Then Charlotte noticed scattered piles of gift wrap all over the floor. They really had missed nearly all of it. She gave her sister an apologetic smile, and Grace returned it warmly.

Sam rushed over to Charlotte, halting before he could run up onto her toes. He held out two presents. "These are for both of you."

"Thank you," Charlotte said. She took the presents and handed Dean the one she recognized since she'd bought it. The other one was from Grace. Charlotte raised her eyebrows at her sister. She'd assumed they would exchange presents in the morning so she'd left her gift for Grace at the cottage.

"It's an extra," Grace said.

Curious, Charlotte opened the present. Inside lay a round, flat ornament painted with a building Charlotte recognized instantly. "My cottage!"

Grace grinned. "I had it made over the summer. I saw a young woman who did the most adorable tiny paintings of local buildings, and I commissioned her to do the cottage."

"I love it," Charlotte said. "But I don't have anything for you tonight."

Grace patted her stomach. "You've given me more than enough delicious food today."

Groans of agreement came from all around the room, making Charlotte's cheeks warm slightly. Cooking for family or for an inn wasn't as prestigious as being a chef at an upscale restaurant in Charleston, but it had its own perks.

Dean nudged her. "Can I open mine now?"

"Have at it," Charlotte said.

He unwrapped the gift, then roared with laughter. The small box contained a recipe card. On the top, it said, *Charlotte's Secret Stuffing* and the rest of the card was blank. "Wow, you know how to hurt a guy," he said, though he was still chuckling.

Charlotte reached over and lifted a piece of foam that filled the bottom of the box. Under it was a gift card to an upscale kitchen store that she loved. She was sure Dean would love it as well.

"Sneaky but I like it," he said. "Thanks. Now you have to open the present from me."

"Where is it?" Charlotte asked. She expected a small box similar to the two they'd just opened, but instead Sarah handed her a large box. "Goodness, what is this?"

"Grace suggested that I get you a present that represents our friendship," Dean said. "And I thought this fit the bill perfectly."

Her curiosity piqued, Charlotte tore the paper from the box. Inside she found Rock 'Em Sock 'Em Robots, a children's game. Charlotte burst out laughing and held the present up so everyone could see.

All around the room people cheered and called out teasing comments.

"Can I play with you?" Sam asked.

Dean raised his hand. "You'll have to wait your turn. No cutting in."

"Oh, you think we should play with this?" Charlotte asked him.

"I thought we could battle over whether you're going to share that stuffing recipe with me," Dean said.

"Battle for the honor of the family," Paisley sang out.

Several others added their agreement.

Charlotte leaned closer to Dean. "That's one battle you'll never win."

Dean hooted. "Sounds like game on to me."

Ricky swept the piles of wrapping paper from a nearby table. "The battleground," he announced.

"I guess we have to give the people what they want," Charlotte said as she carried the game to the table.

Dean settled into the chair across from her. "That's the chef's creed."

The kids in attendance crowded around so close that Charlotte worried a little about accidentally bumping one of them as they battled. To her surprise, the children weren't the only ones to crowd in and cheer while she and Dean wrestled the robots around.

Charlotte felt thoroughly goofy, but she was having a great time anyway.

Finally, Dean wrenched his robot around and managed to sock hers right in the jaw. The robot's head flew upward. "I win!" Dean yelled, jumping to his feet and pumping his fists into the air.

Charlotte was almost glad he'd won, since she suspected she'd have behaved the exact same way and the thought embarrassed her a little. "I'm skeptical because you bought the game. How do I know you didn't rig it before giving it to me?"

"You're clearly trying to weasel out of the deal," Dean said. "Now you have to share the recipe with me."

"Nope," Charlotte said mildly. "We didn't shake on it. And there's the whole business of the game being rigged." She got up primly and headed for the door.

Dean followed her.

Charlotte heard the sound of the robot game being played and knew the kids had jumped in the moment it was free.

She stopped in the doorway and turned to Dean. "Thank you for the game. It was an adorable gift, and I had fun." Then she poked him in the chest with her finger. "But I'm never telling you the stuffing recipe. Now, I need to go check the dessert table and see if it needs replenishing."

Before she could leave the room, Dean stopped her. "I think I ought to get something for winning. After all, it was a strenuous battle."

Charlotte crossed her arms over her chest and regarded him skeptically. "What did you have in mind that isn't a secret recipe?"

Dean grinned, showing off his white, even teeth. He pointed to the doorway above their heads.

Charlotte glanced up and saw that while they were in the kitchen, someone had added a sprig of mistletoe to the greenery over the doorway. "How did you even see that?"

"I'm always searching for interesting new opportunities," Dean replied.

"Opportunities?" she echoed.

"To collect a reward for winning the game," he said. "Fair is fair."

Charlotte sighed dramatically. "I suppose you're right about that."

His grin widened as he slipped an arm around her and pulled her close, trapping her crossed arms between them. Then with his free hand, he tilted her chin up and kissed her, sending the room into wild applause.

To Charlotte's surprise, it wasn't the quick peck between friends she'd been expecting.

To her even greater surprise, she enthusiastically kissed him back.

Then their applause turned to laughter as Jake said, "It's about time!"

And if anyone disagreed, they never said a word.

28

Grace

Grace saw Jake wave in her direction as he stood up from the love seat, giving both Winston and the stuffed reindeer a pat on the head before heading for Grace.

"The party is going great," he said when he reached her.

"I agree." She linked her arm with Jake's. "So are you ready to let me know what's going on with you? And the young lady?"

"I haven't been honest with you," Jake admitted. "In fact, I flat-out lied. I'm so sorry. I'm ready to come clean now. I only met Michelle yesterday, but she is connected to something I need to tell you."

"What is it?" Grace asked, bracing herself for the news.

"I've been offered a job," he answered. "It's a pretty big promotion and a huge pay hike."

Grace blinked as the words sunk in, then squeezed her son's arm. "Oh, that's amazing! Why didn't you tell me sooner? I'm so happy for you. It's about time someone noticed how brilliant you are."

"I don't know about that," Jake said, though he gave his mother a pleased grin. "But the news isn't all good."

Grace's heart dropped. "And what's the bad news?"

"The job is in China," Jake said.

"Congratulations," Grace said, wincing at how strangled her voice sounded. She made an effort to speak normally. "I'm certain it's still a great opportunity."

Clearly Jake saw right through her. He patted her hand on his arm. "It's okay. I'm not going. I told Michelle earlier today and sent the company an official e-mail about it."

Grace felt the pent-up breath rush out and relief flood in. Even so, she felt she had to say, "Are you sure? Are you doing what's best for you? You know I'll be fine."

"Maybe not fine, but I know you'd recover," Jake said. "But I'm still not taking the offer."

"Why not?"

"I love the life I have now. I like my job and the company and the people I work with. If I took the position in China, I would be a supervisor, and that means I'd be doing a lot less hands-on work." Jake shook his head. "That's not me. I have to believe there's more to my career than chasing the most money."

"I see."

"I know this may not be the smartest decision," he went on, "but I think it's the right one for me."

Grace could hear how hard Jake was trying to sound sure of himself, but she could also hear worry. It was obvious that he was hesitant about his decision. She bumped her shoulder against his. "I think you need to open your gift right now."

"You don't have to twist my arm for that," he said with a smile. "But I thought you sent my gift to my apartment in Raleigh."

"I sent one of them." Then Grace patted his arm and slid her own out so she could cross to the Christmas tree. She pulled an envelope from where she'd slipped it into the branches of the tree right next to Jake's RoboGuy ornament.

When she handed Jake the envelope, she said, "I found this in your baby book. When you were born, your dad and I each wrote a single piece of advice for you in the book."

"I remember," he said. "You wrote to trust in God, and Dad wrote to be true to myself."

Grace smiled, glad Jake had committed the advice to memory. She tapped the envelope in his hand. "It took your poor dad the longest time to figure out what to write. Now open this."

Jake pulled out a sheet of paper. "This is Dad's writing. I'd recognize his printing anywhere."

"That's the rough draft of your dad's advice for the baby book," Grace explained. "Read it out loud."

"'I don't care if you're the smartest kid in the class or the best athlete, but if there's a lot of your mom in you, you're sure to be the kindest,'" Jake read. "'As you go through this life, you're going to have to make tough choices. Don't worry if your decisions don't make sense to other people. They don't need to. Sometimes they won't even make sense to you. But if you're true to yourself, you'll always find the right path. It may not be the popular path or the one that makes everyone happy, but it'll be the path you're meant to take.'"

"See?" Grace said softly. "Your dad agrees with you. You made the right decision."

Jake glanced up from the paper, his eyes shining. "Thanks. This is the best present I've ever gotten."

Grace gave him a teasing smile. "Better than the cowboy boots you got when you were five?"

He laughed. "Only a little bit." Then he hugged Grace so hard that she could barely breathe for a moment. But she didn't mind at all.

When Grace stepped back, she regarded her son. "I'm so proud of you. And your dad would be too."

Jake smiled.

Grace turned at the sound of cheers. Sam and Monica were watching Sarah and Ricky play Charlotte's robot game. Grace grinned at their delight, then scanned the room to see how everyone else was enjoying the party.

As Grace looked around the room at her family and friends, her heart overflowed with gratitude. She was so thankful for all the special people in her life and for the opportunity to run the Magnolia Harbor Inn with her sister.

Grace couldn't imagine a better Christmas gift.

Up to this point, we've been doing all the writing. Now it's *your* turn!

Tell us what you think about this book, the characters, the plot, or anything else you'd like to share with us about this series. We can't wait to hear from *you*!

Log on to give us your feedback at:
https://www.surveymonkey.com/r/MagnoliaHarbor

Annie's FICTION